THIS IS YOUR BIKE PLANTS

FANTASTICAL FEMINIST STORIES OF BICYCLING, GARDENS, AND GROWTH

EDITED BY

ELLY BLUE

ELLY BLUE PUBLISHING,
AN IMPRINT OF MICROCOSM PUBLISHING
PORTLAND, OR | CLEVELAND, OH

THIS IS YOUR BIKE ON PLANTS
FANTASTICAL FEMINIST STORIES OF BICYCLING, GARDENS, AND GROWTH

Edited by Elly Blue
All content © its creators, 2024
Final editorial content © Elly Blue, 2024
This edition © Elly Blue Publishing, an imprint of Microcosm Publishing, 2024
First printing, November 12, 2024
All work remains the property of the original creators.
ISBN 9781648412318
This is Microcosm # 840

Elly Blue Publishing, an imprint of Microcosm Publishing
2752 N Williams Ave.
Portland, OR 97227
www.Microcosm.Pub/BikesInSpace

Cover art by Matt Gauck
Design by Joe Biel

This is Bikes in Space Volume 12
For more volumes visit BikesInSpace.com
For more feminist bicycle books and zines visit TakingTheLane.com

All the news that's fit to print at www.Microcosm.Pub/Newsletter

Did you know that you can buy our books directly from us at sliding scale rates? Support a small, independent publisher and pay less than Amazon's price at www.Microcosm.Pub

To join the ranks of high-class stores that feature Microcosm titles, talk to your rep: In the U.S. **COMO** (Atlantic), **ABRAHAM** (Midwest), **BOB BARNETT** (Texas, Oklahoma, Arkansas, Louisiana), **IMPRINT** (Pacific), **TURNAROUND** (UK), **UTP/MANDA** (Canada), **NEWSOUTH** (Australia/New Zealand), **Observatoire** (Africa, Europe), **IPR** (Middle East), **Yvonne Chau** (Southeast Asia), **HarperCollins** (India), **Everest/B.K. Agency** (China), **Tim Burland** (Japan/Korea), and **FAIRE** in the gift trade.

Library of Congress Control Number: 2024033329

ABOUT THE PUBLISHER

Elly Blue Publishing was founded in 2010 to focus on feminist fiction and nonfiction about bicycling. In 2015, Elly Blue Publishing merged to become an imprint of Microcosm Publishing that is still fully managed by Elly Blue.

Microcosm Publishing is Portland's most diversified publishing house and distributor with a focus on the colorful, authentic, and empowering. Our books and zines have put your power in your hands since 1996, equipping readers to make positive changes in their lives and in the world around them. Microcosm emphasizes skill-building, showing hidden histories, and fostering creativity through challenging conventional publishing wisdom with books and bookettes about DIY skills, food, bicycling, gender, self-care, and social justice. What was once a distro and record label started by Joe Biel in a drafty bedroom was selected as *Publisher's Weekly's* fastest growing publisher of 2022 and has become among the oldest independent publishing houses in Portland, OR and Cleveland, OH. We are a politically moderate, centrist publisher in a world that has inched to the right for the past 80 years.

Global labor conditions are bad, and our roots in industrial Cleveland in the 70s and 80s made us appreciate the need to treat workers right. Therefore, our books are MADE IN THE USA

[TABLE OF CONTENTS]

INTRODUCTION

As I write this, spring is turning into summer, and Portland gardens are out of hand. I didn't really notice how lush yards here are and how normal it is to have something other than mowed grass until, in 2002, I went back east for a visit to suburban Connecticut and was surrounded by concrete and lawns again. On a mile-long walk up Whitney Avenue, I was arrested by an anomaly: a small rectangular tomato patch. It stopped me cold. The differences between my old home and my new one were too many to count, but this was a key one—the literal environment.

Portland seemed almost idyllic to me at the time and still does; you can walk down the street and pluck a plum out of a tree, a breath of air taken even a few blocks from a busy road feels clean and fresh, when you leave your house there are other people walking and places to walk to, and, of course, you can bike around most anywhere without the adrenaline rush of being threatened with physical violence by people who in any other context would be pleased to meet you or at least not trying to murder you.

Before I moved west, someone once told me about an architect who used to lecture everyone that the only way to really see a building was to bicycle past it; that was just the right speed for appreciation. I think that places generally have an ideal speed built in; in the suburbs it's all blocky and minimalist, meant to be driven past in a blur and forgotten; dense places like Manhattan are full of details you miss at anything faster than a walk; Portland, relatively low-density, is walkable and (arguably, though people seem miserable doing it) driveable, but it's best taken in by bike, without anywhere urgent to be so you can make frequent stops to catch up with an acquaintance, rummage through a free box, watch the sunset over downtown, or take in someone's captivating garden, complete, if you're lucky, with chickens and goats. Stopping literally to smell roses is a common pastime here.

Gardens and bikes go together. In an era where more and more freedoms are being taken away, the freedom to grow whatever you want and go wherever you want isn't to be taken lightly. And, like bicycling, growing plants feels like one of the most accessible forms of resistance. Growing anything does, really, so long as it takes carbon out of the atmosphere and turns it into oxygen or food or beauty or a functional part of an ecosystem. Give yourself something to take care of. It's an act that requires a future, produces hope, connects with life.

So much science fiction right now has basically given up on Earth; in our imaginations, we're doubling down on technology and manufacturings and exploring alternatives in space. And to get there, we must embark on perilous journeys across an unimaginable distance, with landmarks along the way being months, years, or centuries apart. In two phenomenal debuts, Temi Oh's *Do You Dream of Terra-Two?* and Yume Kitasei's *The Deep Sky*, groups of teenagers, trained from childhood in hyper-competitive boarding schools, embark on journeys to distant galaxies. They and their ships variously crack under the pressures. Neither novel features particularly realistic science, but both, regardless, portray their crews' mission as the longest of odds. Yet, in these worlds, clearly influenced by

Octavia Butler's prescient, gripping 1993 novel *Parable of the Sower*, space is the only chance we have to carry on the stories and generations of human life.

Damn, that's depressing. So let's talk about plants, and landscapes. Imagine that you are proceeding down a spaceship corridor—walking or floating, depending on the science fictional universe you occupy—and through a hatch, where the cold, gray metal walls of the corridor give way to an abundant profusion of plants bursting from hydroponic tubes, vats of algae, humid, oxygenated air, herbal smells, a hint of decay. This is the part of the ship you go to when you need solace, solitude, a place to think and observe and feel comfortable.

Or think of it another way: the greenhouse module is the place with the details. The ones that change every time you come by, that are worth walking through slowly and stopping to examine closely. It's a sharp contrast from the view outside the spaceship, which, like the most depressing interstate highway on the largest scale imaginable and then some, offers no variation. You watch Earth shrink to nothingness, which only takes a few days. Then all you can see are pinpricks of light from the sun and other stars. In interstellar space, the ship is moving faster than any vehicle yet invented, but there is no sense of movement observable to the human eye. As a crew member on this generation ship, your survival depends on the greenhouse in more ways than one—for oxygen and food, but also for a sense of proportion. By corollary, so does the survival of all humanity, because by the time you reach your destination, there may be nobody human left on Earth.

The function of science fiction is to tell us emotional truths couched in the language of cold, hard rationality. Nothing about the science in these books needs to be accurate, and, in fact, I would argue that scientific accuracy is more likely to get in the way of the truths that need to be conveyed. (Look at Neal Stephenson's abominable *Seveneves*, which similarly follows an arc of humans escaping a dying Earth; Stephenson does actually understand the mechanics of spaceflight, and the science in the first part of the book is probably the most factual of any recent novel in the genre . . . and his enthusiastic focus on it thoroughly destroys any emotional resonance the storyline might have had.) It's the contradictions that hold the truths, even. For instance, in both these teens-in-space novels, the teens are chosen by a supposedly objective meritocracy—and the result is an incredibly diverse cast of characters, whereas we know that in reality, the deck would be stacked in favor of those with longstanding family money and power. It's unrealistic, and that makes the emotional truth of this contradiction hit even closer to home: our survival depends on dismantling white supremacy and systems of generational wealth and power. Similarly, with the gardens on the ships— could one small-to-medium-sized room truly provide all the food, fuel, oxygen, and respite that over a dozen people need to survive for 20 years? Probably not, but again, the truth shines through the cracks: our survival right here on Earth depends quite literally on our relationship with the plants around us.

Robin Wall Kimmerer's stupendous science nonfictional *Braiding Sweetgrass* has a chapter urging us all to "become naturalized to place." She describes rehabilitating a pond on her property in upstate New York, transplanting native species in the second-growth forest around it. It's not where she or her family are from, but it's a place she's made her home. She writes:

> After all these generations since Columbus, some of the wisest of Native elders still puzzle over the people who came to our shores. They look at the toll on the land and say, "The problem with these new people is that they don't have both feet on the shore. One is still on the boat. They don't seem to know whether they're staying or not."

Can we U.S. Americans, she goes on to ask, "learn to live here as if we were staying? With both feet on the shore?"

I really loved reading *Do You Dream of Terra-Two?* and *The Deep Sky*. But the tragedy of both of them is how thoroughly they demonstrate the unlikelihood that our technology and resources will get enough humans off the planet to start fresh somewhere else, or that, even if those humans survived the technological odds, they would likely not survive each other or themselves. There's plenty of science showing that the more time we spend driving, the worse off we are; our physical and mental health, our relationships, and our satisfaction with life suffer more with each additional minute of our car commute. You could bet it all on a last-ditch, high-stakes commute to a distant destination. Or you could go for a bike ride admiring the city around us, plant a tomato patch on your suburban lawn, get your produce from a local farm, stick up for local wilderness, stick an avocado seed in a cup of water in your kitchen window and stop to stare as it unfurls.

We've looked at the stars and learned not to limit the size of our dreams. What if we used what we learned there to go all in, both feet on the shore, and decided to live like we are staying?

Elly Blue
Portland, Oregon
June, 2024

FRONDESCENCE
∽ KATHRYN REILLY ∾

Clara had been biking in the deep wilds of the mountains for just over five hours when she came across the body. Nested deep in a copse of evergreen trees, she stood for quite some time, legs locked, breathing heavy, gripping the handlebars tightly, cataloging what her eyes were telling her while trying to get her brain on board. *Not human*, her mind whisper-shouted, *get away. Uncertainty. Danger. Turn around and go.* But she couldn't. The large, obviously trauma-riddled form was mostly decayed, but the most beautiful plants had taken root around, in, and through it. Other-worldly colors, Mozartian patterns, and divergent shapes existed where they shouldn't. In the season where nearly all Earth's plants were dying back, an oasis of sheer, distinctive beauty unfurled before her, dripping in color.

She slowly circled the area, weaving through the mature trees, seeking anything. Approximately 30 meters away, she found a small ship and the path it had cut on its descent. Scarred trees still stood in one of the last old-growth forests, but the crash site betrayed the violence of the landing. Limbs littered the forest floor, testifying to the battle they'd waged as the hull and wings sliced through them like Grace O'Malley's cutlass. One casualty lay wrecked on the forest floor, skeletal limbs pointing accusingly in the direction of the battered ship's remains. But the ravaged limbs boasted new life, succulent-like plants twining among the fallen branches, small florets bubbling across the broken appendages. Large shards from a shattered hatch looked as alien among the ferns and mosses as the large lifeform itself. She knelt to pick up a shard, but the forest protested its loss; the shards themselves had *rooted*. Gently brushing dirt away revealed spider webs of roots pulsing beneath the soil. Examining the ship more closely revealed herbaceous nodes protruding from punctured areas; some nodes were new and only several inches long, but others had transformed to stems with leaves. Hundreds of baby plants emerged from the wreck. Before she could stop herself, her hands pressed the ship's exterior to discover it was mushroom-like—strong as weather-hardened turkey tail fungi. Her close inspection revealed some type of oily residue, something akin to blood perhaps, where the cockpit once was. She noted what must have been a blood trail where unnamed plants grew in patches from the ship to the lifeform's final resting place. Furred, star-shaped leaves the size of sneakers grew on thorned stalks emitting a sweet scent. Clara sent kindness into the universe for the being that had survived the crash but not the injuries sustained from it. Briefly, her mind wondered if it was better to die alone or die with others.

Arriving nearly back from where she'd begun her investigation, she leaned her bike against an old-growth tree before standing opposite the being and really observed. The elements, or perhaps animals, had rent much of the clothing away, revealing a body with more exposed bone than flesh. Yet, some small bits of tendons and skin remained, hanging loose on the bones, nearly opaque and shimmering in the dappled sunlight. Sockets the size and shape of a bell pepper lay deep within the head structure, but where eyes should have been grew moss. She couldn't see any mouth structure, at least in what she assumed was the cranial area. The moss had fully covered the craters and had begun spreading outwards, rhizoids reaching towards the earth.

But it wasn't Earth's moss. Or maybe it was, transformed.

The being had obviously been here long enough for mice to scurry its clothes away to line their dens and for omnivores and carnivores to try a new delicacy. Of the three lower appendages likely used for ambulation, two displayed gnaw marks on the remaining bones. Another displayed a gouge from what looked to be a powerful downward stroke of a beak, or perhaps a talon or claw.

Sighting a sturdy stick, she picked it up and stepped carefully towards the body. With care, she moved the appendages and found the forest already busy claiming them for its own. A trumpet vine wound its way along the outer right appendage's bone, but, crouching down, Clara noticed that the flowers were wrong. Well, perhaps not wrong, but different. *Evolved*, her mind suggested. *The alien plants are allelopathic; their biochemicals are altering our plants; they're evolving them.* The details of the changes came into focus the more she observed: she saw the flowers themselves had elongated and their traditional sunset red and orange hues seemed deeper, more vibrant, and speckled with what looked almost like undulating leopard's spots. Leaning even closer, they smelled not of cotton candy as she'd always recalled from her youth but more so of an astringent: sharp with a tang. In trying to identify the scent, she realized she'd been holding her breath, and she let it whoosh out before scrambling back with a start.

No, her mind said.

Yes, her eyes replied.

She sat for a moment wondering which sense to trust.

Creeping back into her perched position, balancing her weight on the balls of her feet, Clara once again leaned towards the new plant life and took a big inhale, then directed the exhale in the direction of the flowers. They turned, seeking her breath and seemed to breathe it into themselves, sepals swelling like lungs.

So she sat, for however many minutes, moving her head this way and that to test this new theory. Her eyes were right: the flowers sought out her breath like a ballerina chasing an ethereal note through the air.

Clara retreated to her bike and simply lounged against it, resting her head upon the tree behind it, needing something familiar, something trusted, something sturdy, amid the newness. *This ship's design allows it to foster life when its own is over. Their plants thrive on our carbon dioxide. This could be the future.* She'd taken up mountain biking several years ago after reading about forest bathing; it's exactly what she needed most of the time to feel right, to feel alive, to feel okay. So much of the world was out of her control, but not her moments on the mountain; her choices here ensured her survival, and often left the forest a better place since she removed traces of humanity others had left behind. Moving through the forest, navigating obstacles, pushing her strength and endurance all brought a peace she hadn't known she needed. She relied on herself to change punctured tires, to carry her bike over tree-trunk bridges, to problem-solve seemingly impassable obstacles, to build shelters against surprise weather, to handle mishaps as they arose. Clara biked alone, sometimes for days, because she could. Surrounding herself with living entities far older than herself gave her the hope that survival in a world filled with chaos was possible—that humans might just be able to endure what they'd wrought upon the planet and mend it in the process. Somewhere, likely multiple somewheres, were trees that sprouted the exact day she was born. And while she grew surviving the thrum of a technology-driven world, the trees grew, living, witnessing. She hoped for the days when humanity would pull together and slow down. Needing to escape modern messiness, her biking adventures were often days long, pathless among the ferns and forest's silence.

She unpacked her lunch and ate carefully, quietly, reverently. Finishing, she made sure all the reusable containers were perfectly snug within her pack before moving back towards the being's husk. Crouching down by the head, she took a smaller stick and gently moved the moss within the sockets gently. The rhizoids were interlaced and forming a network in the valley of the socket rooting down. Miniature leaves curved along the socket's sides, reaching upwards where the seta supported capsules growing spores. The closer Clara inspected, the more fascinated she became, noticing the tiny details that shouldn't be there but were. This moss, unlike its kin just meters away, seemed to pulse with a faint glow. The setae, instead of slightly bent under the weight of the capsules, were corkscrewed, coiled tightly and rhythmically contracting and expanding: a vertical slinky supporting each rounded capsule. And the capsules, instead of the dusky green of those covering the forest's floor, boasted a vibrant indigo with a sheen that caught the sunlight. Stronger, the setae seemed to support capsules double or triple their regular size. And when she exhaled, they arched towards her, a swan's elegant neck extending, curving towards her every breath.

Bike to help, her mind offered. *Bike until you have a signal and call everyone. The authorities. The journalists. The scientists. Everyone.* She thought about that a bit, eyes roaming over the decaying form, appreciating how the autumnal leaves had begun blanketing it. *In just a few more weeks, the leaves will offer final sanctuary*, she thought. But her brain told her, *But soon, the capsules will burst, and the spores will spread. What will take root? This is not of here; it does not belong. They'll burst in late winter or early spring, and what type of spores will they be? Just what will they become?* her mind reminded, *what then? They will spread and infect the earth.*

"No," she spoke aloud to her mind, "I won't tell anyone. What would they do? They'd come in as a horde, trampling; they'd destroy what's taken root; they'd desecrate this rest. Change can be a gift; the world will be ready for this."

Intent on protecting these altered lives, she congratulated herself for taking wilderness survival courses. She set up camp just a ways away. She rode over the mountain until dusk threatened her vision, scavenging all types of foraged treasure: mushrooms, late berries, chicory roots, greens, wild onions. Settling in, Clara began listening to the forest sink deeper into its evening rhythms, and she planned.

As the stars emerged and the light dimmed, she watched. She watched as the plants that grew from the body without breath seemed to pulse with a faint glow. Like deep sea creatures whose bioluminesce shined, the plants rooted in the body's remnants rivaled the moon's rays, stretching upwards, yearning for the stars.

Closing her eyes, she simply listened. Clara sorted through the noises, organizing them all with ease: the low rustle of tiny paws scurrying, the hoot of a watcher, the whisper of moths' wings; yet, a low, nearly indiscernible rustle eased her eyes open, searching for the sound. She cocked her ear this way and that way until it lined up directly with the body. Something was moving: the mosses and leaves and vines.

The light wasn't just pulsing, the leaves danced with it, and, reaching the surface of bone, they'd bend and sway and brush the sides together, shivering with the sensation in unison like a coordinated symphony drinking in the moonlight.

Clara watched and listened and decided, knowing this single action, the choice before her could alter the world.

In the morning, she rose, dug a hole, answered nature's basic call, covered it up, and then got to work. Survival knife in hand, she approached the ship, intent on helping it fulfill its purpose. If it wasn't a growth medium in and of itself, the ship's design allowed life to begin when it could no longer navigate the stars. She thought of the card she'd received for her birthday containing seeds within the paper itself; during the first good rain, she'd taken the card and planted it. Several weeks later, a riot of flowers blossomed, transforming the postcard of soil into a haven for small lives. Clara was sure if she punctured the ship she could cut away pieces and help them root. Her faith drove the blade into the ship, and it sunk in, like sand falling into the ocean. She worked for days cutting squares and burying them far from the crash site in all directions. Clara sought out shady spots and sunny spots, moist spots and dry spots, leaf detritus and grassy patches—as many different areas as she could to encourage different kinds of growth. Sometimes she swore she heard a square begin to hum. Days evaporated as she biked in the afternoons, finding the new spots to bury the ship's pieces. Returning soaked through, Clara would cut more square-foot pieces before biking farther and farther out to bury the future plants in places of their choosing. Knowing these mountains, she knew discovery was unlikely, but another wanderer like herself didn't need to catch a glimpse of the alien material or unusual patterns and follow their curiosity. In the evenings, she began planning a small shelter and continued to forage.

Tired after a particularly grueling day, Clara placed the final two dozen ship squares in her pack; she would eventually bike them out of the forest and plant each one far from here—perhaps each one in a different state. The more diverse the locations, the harder the change would be to stop. Clara nestled down beside the body; mosses graced not only the sockets, but a long, wide rib-like structure, creating a vast, soft mantle of the new mosses. She curved over it and breathed, watching as the new plants, the evolved versions of themselves infused with something beyond the stars, arched towards her exhaled air. Clara spent long moments simply breathing, slipping into a meditation, watching the hybrids of Earth and somewhere unknown draw towards her. *You breathe me in, I breathe you in. Together. Together.*

Building consumed the next two weeks as the nights chilled; Clara found the tree limbs she needed and built a basic but cozy survival structure. Insulated with moss and camouflaged with brush, she settled in for however long it would take the capsules to open and disperse their spores. Wild mushrooms hung above her head, and a small dugout lined with pebbles hosted her other finds. She spent her days foraging wide and long, drying what she could to save for later and building a wood pile to keep her fire going. She strategically arranged brush and debris around the body to shield it from outside eyes; while the dense evergreen canopy shielded the strange, new botanicals from above, she worked to shield them from the sides.

Every day she checked the body and watched how the plants flourished. They relished the first snowfall, withering not at all. Clara felt the air's chill and the wind's bite, but the plants born into the body of another seemed to mind not at all. She breathed on them, every day, multiple times a day, and witnessed their growth. Against the first snow, the trumpet flowers had grown beyond the size of her head, the vines thick and pulsing with veins of periwinkle light.

In the quiet of simply being, Clara watched creatures come and go. Once-black ravens arrived, feathers shimmering with patterns. Their classic caws seemed more nuanced, musical even. A chipmunk arrived, and she watched as it problem-solved, constructing a solution across a sodden patch of forest floor with a simple bridge. A once-wolf sniffed the air and circled many times before approaching. Violet pupils watched her as he sat, a mere foot away. *Hungry*, she thought, a bit envious of the teal-striped rabbit lolling between his jaws. Cocking his head, his jaws descended, and he left half at her feet before ambling back into the forest. Gratefully, she skinned it, seasoned it with wild herbs, and enjoyed it crispy on a branch.

Days and nights passed as she survived, a witness to the becoming.

And then it happened. One chilly morning, she woke to find an operculum open, capsule yawning wide and spores nowhere to be found.

It was time; they were ready.

She inspected the tiny community and settled on one she thought nearest to opening next, plucked it up, and ate it, relishing the possibility of transformation. Someone always had to be first; today would be her turn.

She broke down her shelter and dispersed the forest back into the forest.

Taking a thin, flat rock, she reverently freed large swaths of the moss with capsules ready to burst from the body and placed them in her mushroom collection bag. Thinner but resolute, Clara knelt by the body and bent low, whispering of the world that could be, thanking the being for bringing her world's new germination. Rising, she settled her pack on her shoulders and looked once more around the old forest, memorizing it. She would no longer live in a world of others' making; she would live in a world remade. Then, grasping the bag full of moss that wasn't quite moss, she biked all over the mountain dispersing spores, hopeful for humanity's future.

THE BICYCLE GROWER

∽ JENNIFER LEE ROSSMAN ∾

My mother used to say everything needs time and patience to grow, even with magic. I've discovered this is especially true for growing a rebellion.

When this was her garden and I was just a little sprout of an elf clinging to her like a tendril to a trellis, the world was a collage of greens and earth tones, the ancient forest standing on tiptoes to touch the impossibly blue sky.

Now it's my garden, and it isn't even mine by law. The earth tones have turned gray like the sky, nature divided into unnaturally square parcels, and the forest is nothing but saplings that will be cut down like their forebears the instant it becomes profitable to do so.

If nothing else, I wish the trees would grow faster. Just so they would block the view of the human settlement looming like a wildfire on the horizon.

Sometimes I'm glad my mother isn't around to see what they've done to us.

Sometimes. Most of the time I just miss her, miss the world I had when she was here and the humans weren't. When the world wasn't perfect but it was safe, when it felt like there was time to be patient and let things grow as languidly as they desired.

∽ • ∾

The human rides straight through the garden, the wheels of his bicycle crushing the fresh green shoots of my chive plants. I should yell at him, nature knows I want to, but if I pass my anger onto him, it will only accomplish adding more chairs to what I already owe.

So I just give him a curt nod in greeting while surreptitiously stealing glances at the gear mechanisms on his wheels, wondering how I could improve the design.

"Ma'am," he says with a nod of his own, resting his bike against my shed and striding past me on his way to the furniture fields.

I follow, as is expected of me, once again marveling at how such a simple machine can save so much energy. He came all the way from the settlement without so much as a drop of sweat on his face.

Just imagine what us elves could do, even scattered across the land as we are, if we could visit each other, communicate, with such ease.

Soon.

"They'll be ready soon," I say, keeping a step behind him as he winds through the rows of small trees in various stages of growth and shaping.

He kicks at one of them with the toe of his boot. For what reason, I can't begin to comprehend, as it can't possibly give him any information about the plant. Must make him feel important. I make a mental note to come back later and set the now-displaced branches back on the form.

"Awful small," the man comments, and then reminds me, "The king is dying."

"The king has been dying for over a decade," I point out, leading him to the proper field, where the thrones for the princess's coronation have been growing since I was a child. "I think he'll hold on for a few more weeks."

"Weeks?"

I cross my arms, my patience waning. "Sir, I intend no disrespect to you or the crown, but I am coaxing the trunk and branches of a tree to grow in the shape of a quite elaborate throne. I will harvest it today if you want, but I will not be held responsible if it collapses beneath the weight of the princess's calcium-rich human bones."

He seems, if not satisfied, at least less irritated at the perceived delay, and turns to leave.

I breathe a sigh of relief. And then he stops, his eyes narrowed at one of the plants in an adjacent field, whiplashing me from relief to anxiety.

"Interesting shape," he says, stepping closer to get a better look at the hickory sapling. It's been curved into a perfect circle, having grown around a barrel which has since been removed, and its branches crisscross each other in the center.

"Experimental design," I lie swiftly, moving so my body blocks his view of the matching wheel. "Maybe a tabletop. Not sure yet. If you're interested, I'll be sure to tell you when it's complete."

The thrones were ready last month. But we weren't.

It feels like it takes forever and a half, walking to every other farm trapped beneath the thumb of the humans. They took our ravens ages ago, when they realized we used them to pass on messages.

Can't rebel if you can't coordinate, can't coordinate if you can't communicate.

My visits are under the guise of delivering seeds, and I suppose that is exactly what I'm doing: helping spread the seeds that will one day grow into something magnificent.

Once I'm back home, I start training the components growing on my windowsill like countless other elves are doing across the land. It becomes a nightly routine, gently coaxing the plants into the shape of the final gears, bending the wood to form delicate but strong teeth to grip and turn the vines that will take the place of the bike chains. It's the same process, with the same windowsill and little ceramic pots, that my mother taught me all those years ago, the same ancient art of furniture growing practiced by countless generations that came before me.

It takes patience, but no part of the plant goes to waste and it produces a more beautiful, natural product than planks of butchered lumber and iron nails could ever hope to achieve.

∽ • ∾

On the day they come to cut down the thrones, I harvest the parts for my bicycle.

The body has been growing the longest, its trunk as thick as my arm with thinner branches curving downward to form the attachments for the wheels and pedals. Though I sand most of it and strip the leaves for practicality, I keep the foliage at the tips of the intricately twisted handlebars. They'll dry eventually, fall off, but they look beautiful right now.

The wheels and gears go on next, each fitting perfectly into place. I hope the others are having as much success as I am; one elf riding up to the human settlement to take back our rights would be as effective as one tree forming an ecosystem.

We need each other to become a forest.

∞ • ∞

Our bikes are crude and primitive, just like the humans say we are. But they're natural and beautiful, just like us.

It may not be much, a dozen elves on wooden bicycles at the settlement gates, but it's something. It shows that no matter what they take away, we'll find a way to take it back.

I know it won't happen overnight. Rebellions, like forests and bicycles, need time and patience to grow.

But today, we are planting the seeds.

BLOOD AND SWEETGRASS
∾ CASS WILKINSON SALDAÑA ∾

An eddy of salty wind caught Pao on their bike. They were exhausted, their defenses low, and so, as the breeze on North Conanicut Island and the howl of full-speed biking mixed together, ready to nudge them off-path, Pao wanted to concede it all. *Sure, let's facedive into the sand.* That's why Pao was there after all—to make peace with pain. To give something of themself away.

Even so, Pao felt their skin ripple with pleasure in the places that touched the air. They did not concuss on the rocks. They crested the next hill and shot through the wind.

Why was it always like this with Pao and biking? Pao didn't understand how the alchemy worked—how on a bike, even lonely and hopeless moments shone like glitter—but it worked. One loop around the island, and the pleasure bloomed. Changed. On the next loop, Pao raised their hands from the handlebars. For a moment, they shut their eyes.

∾ • ∾

"Alchemy" was a watch-word in Pao's family. *You've got bad genes. Alchemy on both sides—the kind of capacity people will devour you to get, if you let them. You can't trust anyone.* Dad had told little Pao that it was their responsibility to maintain discipline in every action—never eating processed grains, never touching a polluted body of water. Three seasons of school athletics to keep Pao focused and distracted. Complete disavowal of all vectors of corruption. Pao felt like they were walking high above the earth on some narrow pass—and that their mother and aunt hadn't made it through. Pao couldn't fall down. There was nothing more repulsive to Pao's father than women *like that*.

But then a fifteen-year-old Pao showed up late one night with a stick-and-poke tattoo hidden on their thigh, the handiwork of their brooding femme crush. It was a silhouette of their first fixie, waggling along a hidden spot of their thigh like a cartoon dog. Nothing enchanted, nothing cursed—just an attempt to look worldly and tough. How could it be too much? The next evening, when Pao had tried to pass through the doorway, the iris door scanner had chirped its rejection—*denied! The owner of those eyeballs cannot enter!*—and Pao had known it was speaking for their father, too. No chance for Pao to explain. Just a door that would never open again.

Now, Pao needed somewhere to sleep—why not the floor of their disgraced Auntie's cabin? If it had to happen, why not get devoured here? A faint voice inside Pao hoped that they were wrong—that the Island could be something entirely different. But Pao didn't dare imagine what that could look like.

Pao opened their eyes. Ahead, like a magic trick, there was Aunt Jade—leading Pao by a good distance but visible in the lull between hills, shooting up the next one and disappearing, until only the shimmering blues and greens of Narragansett Bay remained. Aunt Jade was real. The Wetlands Witch was riding a bike just like Pao's—and she was riding it in strange bursts and angles, utterly unconcerned with cadence and appearance. Fast as hell. Capable enough to devour.

"Ah ha!" Jade shouted. "We got a bird weave! Stable pattern!" She tossed her bike aside.

"Uh, what now, Aunt Jade?" Pao called, cautious, cruising to stop alongside their aunt's bike. But Jade was already flying across the grasses in a dead sprint, crouched low like a shadow of black dress and leather boots, talking quickly to herself. Two hours of biking loops across the island had not worn her down one bit.

∽ • ∾

Aunt Jade was nothing like Pao had imagined. For one thing, she was *fit as fuck*.

When Pao was eight, Pao had found Jade's holohex code deep in the hallway closet, scrawled on a scrap of paper. Pao had recognized Jade's name from one of Dad's lectures—*Dirty punks on that Island call your mom's sister the Wetlands Witch. Out there, anything is fair game. You can't trust freaks like that*—you *in particular. Think what they'd do to you.*

Maybe Pao knew the moment was coming, that they'd never be as exacting and guarded as their father, who always smelled like aftershave and only smiled in a dangerous way that didn't reach his eyes. That something was already in motion to push them off the narrow pass and into a land of *freaks like that*. So Pao had guarded the holohex scrap carefully; when they were old enough, they had committed the code to memory.

In the middle of the night, Jade had picked up. She spoke in quick mumbles. She had bought Pao a solar ferry ticket—the first one out that morning. A few hours later, in the shocking brightness of dawn after a sleepless night, Pao had spotted Aunt Jade on the dock with no trouble—the tall, billowing shadow. She had stood at the dock and strapped the oversized bundle of Pao's belongings onto her cargo bike without complaint, only asking that Pao join the morning's restoration survey, whatever that meant.

That all had to count for something. Pao hoped it did.

Suddenly, Jade yelped in the distance. Pao vaulted their bike frame and ran after the Wetlands Witch.

∽ • ∾

"Uncanny," Jade whispered to herself, peering over the edge of the mound. Against the dune, Jade's silver hair caught the morning sun like fire in an old movie. "Pao," she said, without turning, and Pao realized they had been breathing heavily. Panting. "Aren't you supposed to be the family athlete?" Jade patted the sand next to her and mumbled, "have a rest."

"Low blow, Auntie!" Pao shot back. They hadn't been expecting—what, cockiness? Pao scrambled up the mound, and, to their surprise, Aunt Jade twisted and stuck out her tongue before pivoting back to the water. Up close, Pao could see a series of numbers and geometric diagrams sketched with what looked like a very tiny twig in Jade's fingers.

Pao watched for a moment, baffled.

"You said, 'We got a bird weave,' what, uh, does that mean?" Pao asked. But Jade did not answer. Her scribbles quickened; she seemed to be concentrating with all of her body.

The next time Jade looked up, Pao followed her gaze.

Below, the Narragansett waves lapped water from the western shore into a handful of eastbound creeks. The creeks curled against each other, sometimes merging and separating again, until they passed the crumbled remains of a bridge and met the eastern shoreline. Tall grasses nestled between the curves, and Pao noticed a dozen or so small crabs hiding. To the north and south, the tall grass gave way to a shorter species, with purple and yellow flowers scattered along the fringe of contact.

It was along the meeting point of creek and high marshes that Pao saw three birds flying just above the water. Something in their movement was odd.

"Night herons," Jade said before Pao could look for what it was. "Late morning is just fine for them."

"Are they . . . hunting?" Pao ventured.

"Is that what you see?" Jade laughed.

Pao couldn't make sense of that one. They turned back to study the movement of the birds, which appeared to follow a regular pattern. After a while, Pao understood the *weave* part of *bird weave*—the herons followed the pattern without fail, passing each other and doubling back.

"Aunt Jade—maybe they're looking for fish in the water? Their little circles kind of follow the edges of the creek."

As soon as Pao said it, they realized it was more than following edges—the birds bobbed and flowed in a way that felt *liquid*. How did they coordinate with each other like that? The birds did not seem to be flying so much as carried along a current. Pao squinted again, and this time they jumped. "Holy shit, wait . . . those birds? Are they flying *backwards*?"

Jade jerked her head back at Pao, this time muttering: "People ask such odd questions when they get close to the work." Pao's cheeks grew hot. But Jade had not spoken with malice—to the contrary. Pao realized she was *enjoying* having an audience. How long had it been since somebody had watched Jade at work? Did everyone else on the Island know to keep their distance?

"Pao. I want you to perceive for yourself. To build your own frame of reference."

Jade reached into her satchel and pulled out a compact, angular structure. She tugged at one end and it exploded into a large geometric bag. "Gather some shells for me, young one? Fragments are good. *Big* fragments are best. And only shells with nobody home, please." Okay, Pao thought, something concrete to do. Pao nodded and grabbed the bag, then ran down to the mouth of the tidal marsh.

∾ • ∾

By the time Pao returned, the late morning air had warmed considerably. Pao plopped down the overstuffed bag and wiped sweat from their brow.

Jade tipped the bag over, so that a mini avalanche of shells tumbled to their feet. She crouched down and pulled out a hammer from her satchel. Pao's eyes grew wide as Jade examined her implement, then *very* wide as Jade began swinging the hammer against the shells. *Crack! Crack!*

The bursts of skillful, precise violence made Pao wonder whether Jade was used to taking what she wanted. The thought made Pao squirm. They already knew they'd lose in a dead sprint against their aunt. Is this what giving up a vector of contamination felt like? Pao watched carefully in silence, body tense.

Then Jade did something unexpected—she looked Pao straight in the eyes and said: "Did you know I worked on bikes when I was your age?"

"You did?" Pao was caught off guard.

Jade kept swinging. *Crack! Crack!*

"That's what your mama told me, anyway—that I worked on bikes for the mutual aid network. Said that before the Twin Floods, I was some kind of mobile repairwoman—biking in every kind of weather to fix a jammed gear."

The phrasing was strange. "My mom told you?"

"Yep. She had to—my memories got scrambled when I flew off the bridge in the middle of a hurricane. I was on some kind of repair job—ha! She said I cut my neck on the rocks. Turned out *I* was the repair job."

Crack! As Jade swung the hammer, Pao noticed the keloid scars along her neckline: wide streaks of white that glistened like sediment flecked with mica.

"You have no memory of that at all? Like, my mom filled it all in?" Pao asked, and Jade nodded her head.

"I woke up and parts of me were—well, 'cleared out' isn't the right way to say it. *Changed* in the way a tide rushes in and changes the shore—except some things never changed back. Something was hiding out in the bay. A refugee. Any creature will seek shelter in a storm. It turns out that this particular creature was the type that could seek shelter in a person like us. And you know, we have the type of bodies that don't *close off* unless we want to close off. When we're open, we are a *mineral-rich ecosystem*, you might say."

Jade's sudden use of *we* took Pao aback. What would make Pao and Jade *mineral-rich*? And what kind of creature hides *inside of bodies*?

Jade sighed, like the questions weighed on her, too. "We both should have died. Instead, we took shelter in each other. I suppose you could say we *imprinted* on each other, too."

By now, Jade had pulverized most of the shells into flecks the size of coarse-ground coffee. Tens of thousands of fragments. She looked up at Pao and smiled, "We don't need all of the shells. Just enough to stimulate recognition. Some of me, and some of them."

Jade set the hammer down and picked up a curious rectangle from her bag. She clicked a button on the side, and a thin blade swiped into place.

"Oh fuck!" Pao shouted as Jade dug the switchblade into her palm. Blood bloomed. Jade overturned her hand, so that deep red droplets specked the shell fragments. She massaged the shells in wide arcs with her free hand; soon, the blood intermingled with everything.

Jade scooped up an armful of bloodied shells and headed to the edge of the tidal marsh. She stepped gingerly on damp land—more saltwater than sediment. Pao watched from the grass, frozen.

"Nice to see you, old friend," Jade said, and flung her armful of shells up into the air. The shells rose and glistened: bone white, blood red.

They did not fall back down. Instead, they hovered in the air, until the air itself absorbed the red, like a stain spreading in cloth. Until the air was clearly no longer air.

∽ • ∾

"Holy fucking shit," Pao muttered to themself.

A moment ago, the tidal marsh looked simple: a flat expanse pricked by scattered grasses.

Now, bloody shell specks had dispersed enough to create a meshwork of whites and reds, giving volume and form to what before had looked empty. A pass-through.

No. The air was alive.

Pao made out tendrils—they shot up in all directions. Massive, slender structures. Some snaked to the height of ten humans. The tendrils sprouted from patterns closer to the water that resembled roots—shells in this part of the mesh mixed with algae and bounded between floating leaves, reaching sideways out onto the banks. Touching the crabs and tiny bird feet.

One tendril rose into the air and split into dozens of articulations, each one a distant echo of a finger. These fingers wrapped around the herons, guiding them along the impossible crisscross pattern in the air, like a basket weaver deep in concentration.

Even tens of thousands of shell fragments weren't enough to trace the outlines of every spiral. Smaller specks hovered near the high grasses. The smallest grouping of specks could have belonged to a single tendril, or twenty.

There was a rhythmic gentleness to the way the tendrils moved the birds. For a moment, Pao filled with a sense of the impossible play of movement, of water, of wind. The marsh spoke for itself.

And then Pao looked to Jade—saw the swirling blood that pooled under her fingers, this place where tendrils and blooming blood touched—and something lurched painfully in their chest. It was blood, wasn't it, that made the whole thing possible? Blood that could be used up—taken advantage of? Mined like a *mineral-rich resource*? Invaded, depleted, discarded?

Aunt Jade had let this thing rush inside her. She had given up her memories. And suddenly Pao felt foolish, and small, and the shame from every one of their father's lectures rushed into them at once.

"You want my *blood*?" Pao shouted at Jade with wild eyes.

"Your blood?" Jade said, tilting her head. Behind Jade, the tendrils glistened in the sun, kneading the birds.

"This is what you took me out here to do, isn't it? Feed me to this—" Pao searched for words but instead just waved their hands around.

"Pao. I only wanted to teach—"

"*Fuck* what you wanted! God, I'm so stupid. I'm *fifteen*, I should know better. I thought I could do this. But not like this. I'm so stupid."

Aunt Jade was the same dead end as every adult in Pao's life. Love that came with conditions. It wasn't any different than the locked front door—as soon as Pao fell off the narrow path, they would be discarded. They would be nothing.

Pao turned away and started running through the marshland. They slipped.

Pao screamed. Before they could hit the shimmering sediment, the tendrils drew back. When Pao landed in mud, it was just Pao. Alone.

Jade reached out her arms. But Pao leapt back to their feet.

"No!" Pao yelled, and Jade stopped. "No. I don't care. I'm done. I won't end up like . . . like . . ." Pao fell silent. Wordlessly, they spun around.

Pao ran until they found their bike and scooped it up. Jade didn't give chase after all—just stood there, in her ridiculous black layers, watching Pao bike with every bit of energy in their legs. They needed to leave right now, when their body was still their body, or they might never make it out.

$\infty \cdot \infty$

Pao breathed deep and ragged as they watched the just-missed ferry depart. Another would be leaving in a few hours. Pao walked their bike to the side of the makeshift pier and sat in the sand.

Minutes passed. Ten. Twenty. Pao's mind churned with possibilities, adjustments, calculations.

As the adrenaline of escape left their systems, Pao's thoughts began to crash into one another. They had been awake for too many hours in a row. They didn't want to think. They didn't want to be perceived by anyone. Pao fell asleep.

"Huyo, kid, spare a hand?" said a voice. How long had Pao been out? They groaned and twisted around to find a figure on a bike, towing a cargo trailer—only a figure because they were boxed in on all sides by mounds and mounds of journals and small leather pouches and reed-woven packages, each balanced atop one another in stacks much too high. A single gloved hand attempted to hold the bike steady while another frantically rearranged the items at the top, which looked ready to tumble at any moment.

Pao was familiar with the Balancing Drama of the Cargo Bike; they jumped right up and took the three topmost packages from one stack and placed them to rest on the wooden dock. Now they could see the figure was a courier: a little past middle-aged, with short silver hair, and wearing a sparkling cape over pragmatic, well-worn clothes. No clear gender, or no gender to speak of.

"Thanks! Would've thought I knew better, huh?" the courier winked at Pao. And then looked more closely. "Oh, yo! I saw you this morning. Staying with Jade?"

Without waiting for a reply, the courier ran their hand along the remaining stack and pulled out a large woven bag. "Just her luck! Narragansett Nation herbal plots are coming up lovely. Jade shouldn't have to make do as often. Always good to keep it in-the-Bay, eh?"

Pao looked down at the package in their hands. "I'm, uh. I can't help you. I'm leaving."

The courier looked up at the sky and scratched their neck. "Oh, but we still have a few hours till the next ferry. Plenty of time, yeah?"

"Um." Pao hesitated, then put the package back on the pile and looked at their feet. The courier frowned.

"No time to bring medicine to your elders, huh?" the courier muttered to themself as they picked up the packages and shuffled past. "And to think we'd all be mucking around the bottom of the Bay without Jade."

At this, the courier swung onto their bike. "Mainlanders, never missing a chance to prove ya right . . ."

"Wait," Pao caught up to the courier, breathless. "You said something about the bottom of the Bay?"

The courier turned to Pao and crossed their arms.

"Uh, also. Sorry." Pao added awkwardly. They met the other's eyes. "I'm sorry." The courier slackened their arms.

"The very bottom. Sludgy death."

"Aunt Jade saved you from that?"

The courier looked past Pao, and Pao turned. Beyond the edges of the port, beyond the sand and boardwalks and buildings, a little pop of sharp-green grass pointed out against the water. The very start of the tidal marsh, even out here.

"Look. The Twin Floods messed things up. Deep Oceans know that I lost a screw or two. But nobody changed like Jade. Said the news reports were true about the escaped—what did they call it—the captivate aquatic consciousness from some kind of Navy installation. The UN called us intergalactic criminals. They were right. Anyways. Jade said she met the runaway in the wetlands. Said it was painful, to welcome something that scared in, but then they became like old friends—whatever that means. Nobody believed her. But you know Jade, the funny thing about her, she couldn't care worth a damn for belief. She just wanted to give that creature a home."

"And so this . . . saved the Islands?" Pao asked.

"Oh, we didn't know it back then. Everyone was arguing about whether to build the town back. Same folks who ran away said they needed it back, and they needed it better. Robot-ducts and concrete. A town up in the sky on metal stilts, like a goddamn picture book. But Jade just got out there and, you know, she talked to it. Lord knows how you talk to crabs, but she talked and she listened, and she taught us how to take care. Managed retreat and strategic regrowth and just stuff she did on her own that she never spoke to anyone. None of us met her friend, you know, but we saw the wetlands bounce back. After the families with money gave up and her people went mainlander—her sister was your mom?—well, Jade kind of lost touch with the rest of us. Maybe those screws did come loose."

At this, the courier paused and looked carefully at the marsh. "Jade does good work. Deep Oceans help us. Flood after flood, the tidal marsh soaks up the worst of it. Doesn't die off, you know, just moves. Changes. All I know is, Jade was the first place that runaway found, and she didn't turn it away. Maybe Jade really does care more about that *thing* than us. We got our problems here, that's for sure." The courier paused. "But would it matter any which way?"

Pao took the med package and bolted across the Port. It was the golden hour, and in the long afternoon sun, Pao could see the Port much more clearly than during their predawn arrival. People shouted, passed crates, laughed, argued, pointed at things. Many wore waterproof boots and tall, bright socks. Along with the bikes, Pao saw all kinds of skiffs, rafts, canoes, and a few floating robots. Their vessels flew banners announcing medical aid, and several said "Autonomous Narragansett Nation"; still others had a single, delicious-sounding word, like "Ramen."

In each little interaction, the faces and bodies seemed to communicate a variation of the same idea: *I trust you. I can get my affairs mixed up in yours; that's okay.* A day earlier, when they had a bedroom to return to, they didn't believe a place like this could exist. What felt like shame earlier—the shame of Pao's dad being right—now struck Pao as grief. They didn't believe a place like this could exist.

∾ · ∾

Pao leaned the pouch of medicine against Jade's screen door. In the moonlight, their aunt's cabin looked cozy in its grove of maple trees, snug and surprisingly tall with a high A-frame roof. Pao caught the glow of a solar lamp through an attic-level window. A shadow paced up there, and if Pao strained, they could hear the murmur of Jade's voice: fast and then slow. Like runs in a stream.

The cabin was just a few minutes from the tidal marsh. As Pao rode, their mind moved to the motion, the rush of cooled air. The light from the full moon and stars was just enough to navigate by. Before long, they stood on the dune again. A few of the bloodied shell fragments scattered on the sands and grasses.

Pao paced back and forth, squinting into the water and running a hand through their hair. The marsh was still—or was it?

A few crabs skittered in the tallest grasses.

"I'm not going to, like, bleed for you!" Pao finally shouted. "And my body is mine! No visitors allowed. Got it?"

Pao looked at the crabs, which had paused in their tracks.

"Also, I can't really tell what is you and what is here. Does that question even make sense? I don't fucking care!"

The tidal creeks lapped against a small gathering of muscles, rocks, and sand. Somewhere in the high marsh, an owl hooted.

"It's like," Pao started, and then stopped. "Getting kicked out, you know, it was the end of something bad. All of a sudden, you're free. Maybe you know what that's like. And being free should feel good, you know?" Pao paused.

"But all I can think about is that path high up in the sky. Riding my bike on the very edge, knowing I would fall off. All of that time he said he would protect me—what he really meant was that it would be so fucking easy to throw me away. It would take nothing."

And Pao kept talking. About their dad and that shitty house, the bike leagues and their old fixed-gear frames and tools, playing with their mom when they were young. How good it felt to win a match. Pao talked and talked, and as they did, a breeze kicked up in the tidal marsh. It curled in eddies, and it touched the unseen birds, and it glistened with little bits of starlight. It smelled of salt and sweetgrass. A wisp of breeze curled against Pao's crossed legs, like a dog flopped down in the family living room. Pao felt their shoulders slacken at the touch.

LISA EVER AFTER
✍ ELLA P. FRANCIS ✍

Vasilisa the Wise they called her, though once they had called her Vasilisa the Beautiful. A wistful expression greeted her as she met her own eyes in the mirror. She did not feel particularly wise nor beautiful. "Oh, don't look so pathetic, Lisa," she chided herself. She had taken to using the modern, short version of her name. A suspiciously silver strand of hair curled from under her riding hat. "You've still got it." She forced a smile.

Bluish-purple half-moons puffed under her eyes. Baba Yaga had been visiting her dreams again. Lisa had not told Milos, no need to alarm him. He would only put her back on laudanum for her "hysteria"—as the physicians called it—which made her a veritable zombie. Ever since the accident, she had suffered nightmares about the witch in the forest. Stupid, since everyone knew Baba Yaga was just a story to frighten children.

If only she could recall the accident itself, perhaps then she could make sense of it all. The psychoanalysts Milos had hired spoke of repressed memories and trauma. After her violent reaction to experimental hypnosis, they suggested some things were better left forgotten. They were probably right. Her stepmother and stepsister had been killed in the explosion that incinerated their home. Miraculously, Lisa had been thrown clear of the blast, where she had been found by Prince Milos, who was returning to town late in his steam-powered carriage. He'd brought her to the palace for treatment and recovery. And the rest was history.

She dabbed some chamomile balm, made from herbs in her own garden, under her eyes. The botanical scent, reminiscent of a sunlit field, soothed her soul as well as her skin. Since Milos was away at a steam convention in a neighboring town, her day was her own. She had begged off going, using her health as an excuse, which, while effective, made her cringe. He hadn't put up much of an argument, even seemed relieved—or perhaps that was just her paranoia. She would take her bike out foraging for plants, and then visit her garden. Those two activities, cycling and gardening, always made her feel sane and somehow more alive.

She spun and admired her outfit. Scandalous, they had called it when women started wearing pantaloons, but skirts just weren't practical for cycling. She cinched her belt around her waist and smiled. Regular exercise had kept her trim. She shrugged on the fitted jacket, the puffed sleeves of which accentuated her hourglass silhouette, and buttoned the matching gaiters over her boots and the lower portion of her bloomers. She had designed the ensemble in a bold floral pattern of autumn hues: ochre and saffron with splashes of vermillion. Such riding outfits were all the rage with ladies in the cosmopolitan areas, especially the suffragists.

Milos didn't approve—of the outfit or the suffragists—but after Lady Ana's incident, he stopped protesting her choice of attire. Being exceedingly proper, Ana had insisted on cycling in full skirts, at least until the day the heavy fabric became entwined in the gears and ripped her from her bike. She could not untangle herself and was stuck lying on the cobbled street until scissors could be fetched. It was an hour before she was cut free, and all the while her undergarments had been exposed to the world. Lisa stifled a giggle and admonished herself for finding humor at Ana's expense, but the woman was such a prude at times. After that, Milos worried less about what people thought of his wife's choice of dress since the alternative could be a worse embarrassment to him.

Prince's wife. Lisa snorted. Was that who she was? As a commoner, she couldn't even claim the title "princess." Still, she shouldn't complain about her lavish lifestyle. After all, she had achieved her wildest dreams. Hadn't she? How many low-born girls actually get rescued by their prince and whisked away to his palace? And she had raised a beautiful daughter. Never mind that Mila had run off with that traveling troubadour. Milos had been furious, but Lisa secretly envied her, even though she missed her fiercely. What adventures she must be having. She mentally wished her daughter well and rang the handbell for the butler to ready her bicycle. She would not allow the pang of loss to stifle her mood, not today.

Lisa pedaled along, her tires crunching the gravel. Here the rails were nearly parallel to the road, and she pumped her legs harder, trying to outrun the train chugging up behind her. The modest heels on her boots kept her feet firmly on the pedals, and her gaiters kept her laces safely tucked away, so she was able to work up a good speed without concern. Soon, both her lungs and her thighs began to burn, so she slowed to catch her breath. The train, victorious, clanged on, belching steam and smoke into the sky.

Another cyclist passed her on a white bicycle, dressed all in white. "Good morning!" she called out, but the rider continued on without acknowledgement, and disappeared into the distance like morning mist. "How rude!" What a terribly impractical color for cycling, anyway. She caught herself humming a tune her mother had sung to her as a child.

Early rider clothed in white,

Bringer of the morning light,

Chases darkness from the night.

She turned her bike onto a narrower path which hugged the forest edge. Overhead, the early autumn leaves were still green, but some showed a blush of the color they would become. The undergrowth brimmed with interesting plants. Among them, she hoped to find a rare wild orchid. A patch of dried foliage of the right height and shape caught her eye, so she dismounted and leaned her bike against a convenient birch trunk. She examined the plants near the path, which were, in fact, orchids, but none had seedpods. Unless in danger of destruction, she never uprooted the plants themselves. These seemed safe for the time being.

She spied more of the orchids farther into the woods and stood immobile, rooted to the spot. Fear grappled with her desire for the rare plants. The deep forest haunted her dreams, for it was the abode of Baba Yaga. The space between the tree trunks beckoned to her, daring her to enter into the shadows. Desire for the rare plants eventually overcame her resistance. She stiffened her spine and strode purposely into the underbrush. She would be fine so long as she stayed in sight of the path. "Besides, witches don't exist," she muttered.

Twigs snapped under her feet as she approached the orchids. The desiccated stalks were covered in bean-like pods as yet unopened, still holding their treasure. She smiled in satisfaction and collected a few from each plant, leaving plenty behind to reseed themselves. As she was tucking the crackling pods into her knapsack, a cold breeze rustled through the leaves. "Vasilisa," the leaves seemed to say. "Lisa," they whispered, in an old woman's voice.

Spooked, she bolted toward her bike, trampling unseen anything in her path. She had wandered deeper than she realized. "It's just your imagination," she reassured herself. "Just the wind." But she shivered though the day was warm, and her hands shook as she strapped her pack onto the rack of her bike. She wheeled around and rode toward the village. Maybe I should take my medication. Maybe I am crazy.

By the time she neared her destination, she had calmed down, even laughing at her fear. She entered through the north gate and bumped along on the cobbled street, finally pulling into the yard of her childhood home. Once the property had been isolated at the edge of the woods, but the town had grown to engulf it, and the forest had receded. It was hers now, after the death of her father. All traces of the accident were long gone. She had remodeled the burnt-out remains into a shed and greenhouse and begun to plant her gardens here.

The cottage had been small for a house, but was an excellent size for its current use. Much to the royal gardener's relief, she was no longer messing up his neat rows and planting weeds among his prize flowers. Well, she supposed they were actually her prize flowers, or perhaps Milos's. Still, life was better without the friction. She surveyed her sprawling, haphazard gardens brimming with wild plants and was pleased. Here she was relaxed and at peace. Perhaps this was her way of metaphorically taming the forest, one plant at a time. Or perhaps that was overthinking it. Regardless, she felt she was filling some small purpose in the world by propagating these specimens.

Her parents' graves were nestled among the shrubbery at the rear of the property. She knelt by each to pay her respects. She had insisted her father be buried here beside her mother rather than at the chapel with her stepmother. She recalled her mother singing to her when she was very young, but the memories closer to her death were hazy. Her father had passed much later. He had luckily been away peddling goods in a neighboring town when his new wife and stepdaughters had perished in the accident. After his return, he lived at the palace until his death a few years ago. She missed them both but felt their presence here, in a small way.

A rosebush with petals as red as blood bloomed beside the shed, even throughout the frigid winter-times. No one could recall when it had first appeared or who had planted it. Lisa plucked one of the blooms, mindful of the sharp thorns. It withered in her hands. Such a strange, beautiful plant. She hung her orchid seeds from the rafters inside, where they could overwinter in the cold but be free of vermin. Returning to the rosebush with her gardening gloves and tools, she raked the mulch beneath to expose the soil. Just as she was about to throw a shovelful of compost onto the roots, she noticed a bit of metal sticking out of the ground. She leaned closer. It looked pointed, like the corner of a box.

That's odd. She grasped the object and wiggled it, but it wouldn't budge. She shoveled around the edges, trying to get leverage. Finally, it lifted out of the soil. It was a box, a metal chest she had never seen before. Perhaps the cycles of freezing and thawing had lifted it to the surface. There was a lock on the front, but years underground had rusted it nearly through. A few whacks with the shovel and it fell away, along with much of the box. She pulled out the contents and froze. A burnt cinder of a doll, barely recognizable yet achingly familiar, lay in her hands.

∿ • ∿

"Daughter, you must listen to me," her mother had said. "I don't have much time left." She had pulled the doll from under her bed covers. "Take this and hide it. Show it to no one, not even your father. You must promise."

"I promise, Mama," Vasilisa had said, her lip quivering. "But why—"

"Hush and listen." Her mother closed her eyes for a moment before continuing. "When you are lonely or have need, feed this little doll. Look after her and she will look after you . . . when I cannot any longer."

"But Mama—"

"Shhhh. Come here beside me and let me hold you," her mother had said, patting the bed.

Vasilisa put the doll in the pocket of her dress and snuggled into her mother's side.

∿ • ∿

Lisa stared at the disfigured doll. Its hair, face, and clothing were burnt away. She must have been in the accident, but who buried her here? She sank down onto a stool as memories flooded her mind.

The little doll had helped her through hardships, just as her mother had said it would. Her father remarried quickly after her mother's death. Her stepmother had been a cruel woman who encouraged her daughters to be cruel as well. They taunted Vasilisa terribly when her father was away, which was often, and forced her to do the brunt of the household chores. But each night, after everyone else had gone to bed, she fed a bit of her dinner to the magical doll, and in the morning, the chores would be done.

The mistreatment escalated, until the night that her stepmother claimed that all of the candles were used up and sent her into the forest to fetch light for the house. She was to find Baba Yaga and beg her for assistance. Her stepsisters delighted in telling her terrible tales of how the old witch cooked and ate those who dared trespass in her domain. Having nowhere else to go, she set off into the woods, clutching her doll hidden in an inside pocket. She found Baba Yaga and completed all of the impossible tasks set before her with the secret help of her magic doll. And she was rewarded with a skull torch with glowing eyes. But when she brought it home, her world exploded . . .

Lisa shook her head to clear it and dropped the doll to the ground. No! This couldn't be right. This was her nightmare, not memories. She ran to her mother's grave. "Mama! What is the truth? What is real?" Her mother didn't answer, of course, she was dead. But maybe she wouldn't have been much help alive, either. Papa had told her that her mother suffered from hysteria as well.

She strode back over to where the doll had fallen, half expecting nothing to be there. But there it lay face-down in the leaf litter. She picked it up and brushed it off. It was solid in her hands. If this was real, then perhaps the rest was too. She must seek out the old witch to find out. And if there was no Baba Yaga? Well, that would be a revelation too. She cradled the doll stub to her chest.

As she neared the area where the trees had called to her that morning, a speeding cyclist cut across her path in a flash of red. She slammed on her brakes, just managing not to fly headfirst over the handlebars. After shouting some very unladylike expletives, she noticed that he had taken a nearly hidden path into the woods. Not much more than a deer track, really. Had it not been for the near collision, she would have missed it altogether.

> *Midday rider dressed in red,*
> *Noontime sun above his head,*
> *Announces that the morning's dead.*

She turned onto the trail in time to see the rider far ahead, his red clothing contrasting sharply against the deep green of the spruces. She pedaled faster but could not gain on him. Nor did she fall behind as she coasted to rest her legs. She tested this anomaly over and over with the same result.

Hours passed with the autumn sun dappling the ground where it penetrated through the forest canopy.

Gradually, the shadows grew longer, reaching toward her, then stretching beyond. Sweat trickled down her back and her legs shook from exertion. She stopped in a small clearing and took a long drink from the spring that bubbled there. When she finished, the red rider had vanished. She was alone amidst the jagged stumps of trees thrusting from the ground like tombstones.

Sinking down onto one that was not too pointy, she took out the little doll and offered it a crust of bread. Nothing. Perhaps its magic was destroyed by the fire. Or perhaps her memories were just a hallucination. She put the doll away and ate the bread herself, her mind chewing as much as her mouth. The riders could not be a coincidence. The old tales often associated the colorful characters with Baba Yaga, either as messengers or minions.

The sky purpled and the shadows grew deep. She looked around, not sure from which direction she came, nor which one to follow. All paths looked the same. As if on cue, a black bicycle wheeled across the clearing and down the trail to her right, the rider's black raiment swallowed up by the gloom.

Evening rider all in black,

Captures daylight in his sack,

Takes it to the old hag's shack.

At least she knew the direction now. She picked her way carefully along the trail, pushing her bike because it was getting hard to see where she was going. Something white gleamed in the moonlight ahead that was not birch trunks.

She threaded among the debris to get closer, and could soon discern a fence constructed of bones topped by human skulls. She shivered, just as the black rider leaped over a pile of brush, skidded sideways in a patch of sawdust, and sped off. Night fell like a curtain, and the skulls flared to light. The flames flickering in their eyes making the bone shadows dance. Lisa leaned her bike against the grisly fence and approached the gate with a heart made of lead. She patted the doll hidden in her jacket pocket for comfort. The finger-bone latch released with a click, and Lisa walked into her nightmare.

The gate crashed shut behind her, and the skulls laughed and chattered their teeth. Her legs shook, and she would have run if there were anyplace to go. She steadied her breath and surveyed the scene before her. A wooden shack tottered about on chicken legs, just as she remembered. Except as she looked closer, she saw they were not chicken legs at all but two giant roots sprouting from the bottom of the structure and dividing into toe-like growths, not unlike a chicken's foot in form. As she watched, the appendages lengthened and burrowed into the earth, anchoring the house to the ground.

Vines wriggled away from her feet, clearing a path. She crept forward, her curiosity beginning to outweigh her fear. More roots thickened into stairs and scrolled into railings, leading upward. She ascended and knocked once, twice, three times. The door flew open, revealing a murky interior. She stepped into the gloom and glanced around the seemingly empty space. Steam curled from a black cauldron on the stone hearth. Fragrant herbs hung in bunches from hooks. A wooden trestle table and bench rested along the far wall, and a barrel occupied one corner.

"So, we meet again, Vasilisa," a voice crackled behind her. "That's some outfit!"

"It's Lisa now," she said, surprised at the assertiveness in her voice. She turned but saw no one. "Show yourself, witch."

A hunched figure materialized, unremarkable save for the eerie light in her eyes. "I was beginning to think you would never come," she creaked.

"I am here now. And I have questions."

"And I have answers if you are ready to hear them."

Lisa's confidence wavered.

"But it is late and an old woman needs her rest. Be my guest tonight, and we can chat at our leisure tomorrow. We have much to discuss."

Lisa was suspicious—the old witch was a trickster by nature. But she had come this far, and she was not about to leave without answers. Besides, it was not likely that she would be allowed to simply leave. She would play along for now. The old woman led her into a side room containing a cot and lavender-scented linens. She put on the soft cotton nightgown provided for her and lay down. She had no intention of falling asleep, but it wouldn't hurt to close her eyes for just a few moments.

Despite her resolve to remain awake, Lisa slept, and slept well, with no hint of nightmares. She supposed that was because the witch already had her in her grasp. It did feel wonderful to be refreshed. She dressed in her riding outfit, which had been laundered while she slept. She panicked when she found her jacket pocket empty, but then remembered she had stashed the doll under her pillow for safety and retrieved it. She wandered out to the table and found a bowl of oatmeal with strawberries and maple syrup set out for her. When she finished devouring it, Baba Yaga appeared.

"Shall we get going?" the old woman asked. "There is much I'd like to show you."

Lisa warily nodded. She could ask her questions later.

The roof slid open and tendrils sprouted from the walls and reached into the sky, unfurling huge leaves which caught the wind. Lisa braced herself as the structure lurched to one side, then the other, and began to lift into the air. A panel of the wall slid open, and she stepped closer for a better view, but not so close that she could fall out. The ground drifted away until she was looking down at the tops of trees, waving like blades of grass in a field as they passed.

"This," Baba Yaga said, gesturing to the forest, "is my garden." Her white tresses glinted in the sunlight, and for a moment she seemed to stand much taller and straighter. But soon they drifted over a barren area where felled trees lay scattered across the landscape, and the witch seemed to shrink again. People, made tiny by distance, labored below, cutting and stacking the timber. None of them looked up.

"Can't they see us?" Lisa asked.

Baba Yaga shrugged. "People see what they expect to see. Most are blind to the miracles around them." She looked deeply into Lisa's eyes. "But you are not like them. You are more like me."

"I am nothing like you!" Lisa growled.

"Are you not?"

"You killed my stepsisters and stepmother."

"Death comes to us all sooner or later." The old woman shrugged. "But I assure you it was not me who killed them."

"The light you gave me was cursed. When I brought it home it exploded and killed them."

"And yet you suffered no harm? Did you never wonder about that?"

"What do you mean?"

"All those years ago, you came to me and asked for my aid. You passed my trials with the help of your little doll. Did you think I didn't know? And in return I gave you what you asked. A light, nothing more."

"You lie. It was a trick!"

"Granted, the skull torch was a bit macabre. A dark joke on my part." She chortled.

"It was no joke to me!"

"No, you were deathly serious, weren't you, my dear?"

A chill crawled up Lisa's back. "I don't understand."

"Don't you? All those years you whispered your desires to your little doll. You fed her, and she took care of things for you. How many times did you tell her of your anger at your stepmother? Your stepsisters? Of your desire for revenge?"

"Shut up!"

"And did you tell her how you dreamed of a life of luxury? Hmm? Did you wish for a prince?"

Lisa's rage boiled over. She shoved Baba Yaga with all her strength. The old woman looked startled for a moment as she stumbled backwards, then she smiled smugly as she fell out of the hatch. Horrified, Lisa ran to the opening and looked down. At first, she saw nothing but the blurred landscape below. Then movement to her right drew her attention. A vine was snaking its way around the side of the hut with the old woman firmly entwined in its tendrils. Lisa pulled her back in when she reached the door.

"And do you still think you don't have the propensity for violence?"

Lisa stepped back. "You are twisting my thoughts. Confusing me."

"If you don't believe me, take a sip from the water of life." She gestured toward the burbling barrel in the corner.

Lisa shook her head. She did not trust the witch..

Baba Yaga took a wooden dipper from a hook on the wall and drank from the barrel. "See, nothing to worry about."

"You could still be tricking me," Lisa insisted.

"Perhaps. But what would I gain? If I wanted to kill you I could do so easily at any time. The question is, child, what do you have to lose?"

Lisa sputtered as she couldn't think of a response.

"Come dear. The truth never killed anyone. It will be easier for you to see for yourself than for me to convince you."

Lisa took the offered dipper and sipped a tiny amount of water. It was as cold as winter frost and tasted of nothing . . . and everything. She saw many conflicting things and knew them to be true. She saw that there had been many Baba Yagas over the years, and only one. She saw the sprouting of the first seed on Earth and the death of the last tree. She saw the love in her mother's smile as she made a doll with her own hands and some of Lisa's hair. She saw her father bury that same doll, charred by fire. She saw Milos in the embrace of another woman and knew she had lost him long ago. Finally, she collapsed to the floor under the weight of it all.

She sobbed as frail arms rocked her. She wept for the pain of her childhood and the loss of her mother. She wept for the cruelty of humans and the destruction of the earth's living things. She even wept for her stepsisters and stepmother who had been trapped in their own ignorance and hate. And lastly, for her father who failed to protect her from much abuse.

As the tears ran dry she became aware of a soothing voice. "You must forgive yourself, child, you did not know your power. You were too immature to control your anger. And who could blame you, really."

She looked into Baba Yaga's face and wondered how she had ever found the old woman ugly. Her eyes were a deep-set green, like hidden pools of unfathomable depth. The furrowed lines of her skin like grains in fine wood, etched by experience. And in that face, she recognized an older version of her mother's, and her own. And knew that she herself would be beautiful at all stages of her life, just as she was now.

The old woman continued, "I have been trying to reach you for a very long time, but you were shielded from me by drugs and self-doubt. Finally, I felt your mind begin to clear, and I began again in earnest. I even sent my riders out, in between their other duties."

"And here I am. But why?"

"Over the ages, I have been revered as many things: The Bringer of Life and Guardian of the Dead. Mother Nature and Mistress of Beasts. Though lately, I am simply known as the old hag of the forest, Baba Yaga. But all things must return to the earth from whence they sprang. My time has come."

"No!"

"But decay always generates rebirth. Ever since you appeared on my doorstep clutching your doll, I knew you were the one to take my place." The old woman sighed. "You looked so much like your mother when she was that age."

"I couldn't. I wouldn't know what to do."

"You have all you need here." She waved her arm in a circular pattern to encompass the hut. "But it has to be your choice. Should you wish to return to your old life, simply drink from the Water of Death. You will forget everything." She pointed to a barrel on the other side of the room which Lisa had not noticed before.

Lisa stood and helped the old lady to her feet. "How do we do this?"

"You're sure? There is no going back once the decision is made."

"I'm sure, Grandmother."

Baba Yaga grasped Lisa's hands and began to hum—a sound not unlike the buzz of bees on a warm summer day. Lights reminiscent of the aurora borealis began to flicker about them as a tingling energy surged between them. Lightning flashed, and with a boom, Lisa was left holding a bundle of flowering vines and twigs. Though she could no longer see Baba Yaga, she felt her essence within.

THE CROOKED TREE OF ALGRÜSTI
∽ AMANDA MCNEIL ∾

C elosia leans into the biting wind stabbing at her face with tiny pinpricks of sleet and pedals harder. The faster she can move these wheels the sooner she'll be up this hill and can coast down the other side. The wind will still be biting. With a rocky, icy tundra on one side and the sea on the other, there's nothing to slow it. If anything, it feels like the entire planet seeks to create it. But, at least when she's coasting, she won't be actively fighting it either.

She tries to reframe the unexpected direction her afternoon has taken into gratitude. Celosia six months ago couldn't have responded so rapidly to a request for help. Of course, would anyone have bothered six months ago? She frowns as she crests the hill. When she requested a one-way ticket to Planet Algrüsti, the ticket agent questioned her, "You sure about that, honey? There's," he chuckled, "well there's just not an awful lot there. Besides ice, snow, rocks," he glanced back down at his Mosspad, which formed an emoji and winked at him. "Oh, and there are fewer than 1,000 people on the whole planet."

"That's part of the appeal," Celosia muttered.

The ticket agent, who clearly was an extrovert well suited for the job, closed his mouth and ran a finger over the Mosspad. A piece of parchment emerged. "Fair enough. Here's your one-way ticket."

When the wind bites her face, Celosia misses Planet Viaria's heat, dustiness, and the many adobe buildings with streets full of people. But she does not miss the KreaturFreundin that cannot survive here. They thrive easily on other planets, especially the forest ones, and do almost as well on Viaria, just needing regular misting. Here, no one can even manage to have a Mort. The first humans brought them, but they shriveled away to bare-stemmed nothings. Thankfully, they were brought off-world in time to be saved. But no more are allowed on. So everyone bicycles. Just like her. She no longer stands out.

She tips forward and starts to take the road's downward curve following the coastline. It's breathtakingly beautiful, that's fair enough to say. And it does have life of its own. Fish and the predators that stalk them along the coast and out on the ice. Great, furry, lumbering things that yip late at night at the three moons. Celosia sympathizes. That's when she most wants to cry also. The intrepid locals have begun calling them Nomorts—a play on how much they look like the KreaturFreundin bred to cart humans around. Yet, they are entirely different from them. They're mammalians, not related to plants. They're also possibly dangerous, unlike Morts.

A pang stabs at Celosia's heart as she leans into a left curve about two-thirds of the way down the hill. She blinks back what she tries to tell herself is sleet getting into her eyes but what she knows are tears. She does miss the KreaturFreundin she grew up with. The ones unique to Viaria too. But most of all, she misses her own Mort. Tears threaten her eyes, and she rapidly blinks them away. But she doesn't deserve another Mort. Ever. She never deserved that one to begin with.

Even though she's already got quite a lot of speed from this downhill, she moves up her gears and pedals harder. Her tires skid beneath her as she takes a right-hand curve at the bottom of the hill. The road suddenly straightens out into a flat expanse with another craggy hill looming up on the other side of it. Halfway through the flat, to the right of the road, is a path. She turns onto it, her wheels rattling her teeth as she goes over the paving stones. It's not the smooth surface the main road was. Hazel's house sits in front of her. It reminds her of the homes on forest planets. Two stories instead of the usual Algrüsti one. Full of angles instead of curves. The only real difference is this home is made of brick instead of looming up as a living part of the landscape. It's almost like someone picked up their home from another planet and dropped it here without any regard for the local way of doing things. In a way, that does seem just like Hazel.

Celosia places her bicycle in the nearby domed bike shed, ensures the door latches behind her, then walks up the porch steps. She knocks on the door.

Hazel opens it mere moments later. Her round face is tight and tear streaked. "Come in, come in."

Celosia walks in and nearly trips over Hazel's two overflowing bags. Hazel pulls her into a hug that nearly pins her arms to her sides, but she's just able to lift up her forearms enough to pat both of her hands on Hazel's back. She's glad she managed it because the patting seems to work like an eject button, and Hazel releases her.

"The bereavement committee sped up the departure of the interplanetary transit for me, so they're coming today."

"So you said."

Thank the moons the Mosspads are able to survive here, or the solitariness would be too risky for settlement to have been allowed. They do require careful caretaking though. Misting. Special boxes next to heating sources and heating pads when you go out. She spots Hazel's Mosspad waiting in just such a heated box beside the door, and low-level panic turns her lower stomach into knots. She takes her bag off her back and pats it, checking for her own Mosspad. There's the rectangular shape. It's likely okay, but . . .

"Go ahead and put it by the fire." Hazel gestures at an empty nook. A part of Celosia tells her she should be entirely focused on Hazel right now, but keeping a Mosspad alive on Algrüsti takes precedence pretty much always. She's still amazed she's managed it so far. So she sets hers up in the nook while Hazel finishes packing her own away. She reaches toward its mossy edges to brush it, but stops just short of touching it. She wants to murmur to it, but she hasn't done that since before. . . . She straightens, pulling herself away from both her Mosspad and the thought.

Celosia unzips her jacket and shrugs out of it. Hazel reaches for it. "I love this jacket."

"That's what you told me the day we met."

Hazel smiles, deepening her crow's feet. Her heavy black eyeliner must be waterproof because it is still perfectly applied around her eyes. "You really didn't want to talk," she laughs.

"I just . . . didn't think we'd have that much in common," she responds as she allows Hazel to take her jacket and hang it on one of the guest hooks.

"What? Two of the only people younger than 45 on a retirement destination planet? You're right. What could we possibly have in common," Hazel deadpans.

Celosia nibbles at her lip, looks at Hazel, then away. "You just seemed so cool. Like someone I'd have seen outside a punk rock venue."

Hazel throws her head back and laughs. "Oh, thank you for that. I needed that today. Me, a lifelong admin. Cool."

Celosia walks up to her. "You are, lady. Everything about you is. From your fashion to your nonprofit work to your early retirement on one of the weirdest—"

"Most unique," Hazel interrupts.

"Most unique," Celosia amends, "planets in the solar system."

Hazel grabs Celosia's hands and gives them a squeeze. It's even more uncomfortable than such gestures usually are thanks to the dozens of rings with funky stone settings Hazel wears. Hazel's Mosspad makes a rustle, and she releases her to go read the alert.

"That's the reminder I set to keep myself on schedule. I don't have time to go over everything in detail, but I've written it all down on a piece of parchment in the kitchen," Hazel gestures toward the door. No open floor plans here. Too difficult to heat. Celosia approaches her, gently laying one hand on each bicep. She doesn't love touching people, but she does it when it's needed. And it's needed now.

"I've got it, Hazel. Just go see your father."

Hazel bites her lip.

Celosia never thought she would feel grateful for having experienced her own father's passing but now a flicker of that goes through her. "Even if he ends up not okay, you'll be okay." She squeezes Hazel's arms, and Hazel nods, then glances down.

"I should've retired nearer to him."

"You have to live your own life. And it's not your fault if you don't make it there in time, okay? You can only do what you can do." She gives one more squeeze, then releases her.

"Thank you," Hazel murmurs. "It means so much to me . . . we only met a few weeks ago, and you're helping me so much."

"Celosia looks down at her shoes. "You've been very kind and welcoming to me, in spite of . . ." She's not sure how to finish this sentence.

Hazel doesn't let her anyway, interrupting, "In spite of what? You being human? And a kind one at that."

Celosia looks down, unable to take the compliment but also, at least, able to not reject it outright.

"Anyway," Hazel continues, "I really do have to be off. I don't want to keep the ship waiting after they sped up its arrival for me."

And so, in a whirling dervish of coats and bags and more hugging, she's out the door. Celosia steps out briefly behind her and watches as she gets her bicycle out of the shed, then turns to wave. Celosia remains on the porch, watching as Hazel turns right to continue along the flat further toward the next hill that leads into town.

Celosia closes the tall wooden door behind her and leans against it. The house aches with Hazel's absence. Up until this point, concern about succeeding at such a departure from her routine for days on end hasn't had space to take up residence in her brain. It was entirely focused on Hazel and her needs. Well, entirely isn't a fair word. Majorly. Mostly. At the back of her mind, as she packed her bag and climbed on her bike to come here . . . no, even before that, when she read the message on her Mosspad. A small whisper in her brain. *Is it safe for you to do that?*

Well, she departed from her routine severely in coming here, going in direct contrast to all of the recovery advice she was able to find in any book—not to make any serious life changes within the first year. And what did Celosia do? Move planets. So she can handle a small day-to-day change in routine. She stands up and straightens her shoulders. Her Mosspad rustles. She goes to it.

A message from Hazel. She must have programmed it to arrive when she left. It starts with an exuberant thank-you, then moves along to the list of chores to keep the house secure while she's away. The odd thing, though, is the note at the bottom.

More instructions in the solarium!

The . . . what now? Celosia furrows her brow and moves to the kitchen. There's a door at the back. If it wasn't for the note, she'd assume it was a pantry. She places her hand on the ornate metal doorknob and recoils. The knob is warm to the touch. She reaches for it again, turns it, and opens it.

Before her is a small room. From floor to ceiling are windows. And throughout the room are plants and KreaturFreundin. Sitting on the top of a shelf in the middle of the room is a cylindrical Vibratium with its usual combination of moss and tightly wound vines with medium-sized deep purple leaves in the shape of eighth notes. Bred to create music for any situation, it starts making an ominous noise.

"Afraid of me already?" she asks, but then she realizes she's standing with the door open, letting the heat out. A large thermometer in the middle of the solarium is dropping in temperature already. She steps inside and pulls the door shut firmly behind her. The Vibratium abruptly adapts with what Celosia can only describe as classic elevator Muzak. "Still deciding what you think of me, huh?" The Vibratium, of course, doesn't answer. But it also doesn't change tunes.

Celosia looks around the room. Greenery stretches from floor to ceiling in all types of different pots and containers from many planets. She recognizes a forest-planet style burnt wood one and a terracotta one from Viaria. Some of them are KreaturFreundin and some are plants. Slightly more plants than KreaturFreundin. She recognizes tropical plants like a monstera with its classic Swiss-cheese leaves. And a bird-of-paradise in bloom, the bright orange tufts sticking up from its green leaves. There's a terrarium in one corner that holds the cacti and succulents of the desert. Inside, a rare thimble cactus, with its narrow spires and tiny yet sharp thorns, leans over dramatically. It's getting ready to touch down and start pups. Next to it is a less rare but still beautiful aloe plant.

Written on the window in paint is a caretaking list with tasks that must be done every day as well as tasks done once a week but on different days. "That makes sense," Celosia murmurs, "spread out the work." The only thing is, she doesn't know whether Hazel did these things before she left or not.

This planet has two suns to go with its three moons, and they form an *X* in the sky as they progress. It means every window is a light facing one. You'd think with that much sun the planet wouldn't be icy, but the suns are far enough away that that's not the case. It does make for extra light, which is nice, though. Celosia glances past the fronds and sees one of the suns beginning to set. She considers the angle of the house and decides it must be Sol. Pol is also slightly less bright.

At this moment, a Solstera illuminates itself. It must have sensed the impending darkness as well. Celosia stares at it. This is a rare version of the KreaturFreundin. Its tight brown branches with green leaves the size of her pinky finger twist into what looks like a strand of DNA, and the light emitting from inside of it gives off a bluish glow that lights up Celosia's face as she leans down to gaze at it. She hears a small hum coming from it.

The Vibratium changes tune, shifting into a classic jazz piece. It jars her out of her admiration. Instead, a tight fist clamps down on her chest as the flashback that's been wanting to take her ever since she saw Hazel's message on her Mosspad finally does.

$\backsim$ • $\backsim$

She's again at the moment, just a little more than six months ago, when her bleary eyes focused on her Mosspad, which was a bit brown around the edges—a visible sign of how she struggled to remember to mist it. It displayed two messages.

At the bottom: *Your father required emergency services. This is his neighbor. Come quickly. He might not make it.*

At the top, timestamped fourteen hours later: *I'm sorry to say your father has passed away. Please come home as soon as you can to deal with his estate. We are all sorry for your loss.*

She'd been on a bender right around the time the first message came in. It had started with her cracking open an alcopop, telling herself it was an end-of-the-workweek treat to have with dinner. But then it morphed into opening a bottle of wine. Then she pulled the liquor out of the freezer and just drank that straight. It was fruit flavored, so she told herself that was the way it was meant to be drunk. What did she do in that hazy time when her father laid on the cusp of death with emergency services trying to bring him back? She can't even remember.

It was probably much like what she usually did. Wind her record player over and over again to play the same side of the record, forgetting that she'd just listened to it. Unable to ask a Vibratium to play music for her because she'd sold hers to get money for more alcohol. It was for the best anyway. Celosia had started to notice how plants and, yes, KreaturFreundin struggled to live around her. She joked she had a brown thumb. But she only made that joke to herself.

A numbness had taken over her body. It was a lot like being drunk, actually, except she painfully could remember every single moment of it. Stumbling around her flat packing a bag. Dressing. Leaving without cleaning up anything. Without showering. Racing down the hall to the elevator, then the shared solarium beside her building. Her neighbor's scowl as she unlocked the gate to her Mort. Her neighbor who didn't know what she was going through and decided now was the time to say it: "You really should take better care of your Mort, you know."

Celosia looked inside the yard. Her Mort sat inside. She'd jokingly named her Morticia and then learned that was one of the most common Mort names, but it was too late to change it. Celosia hated being like other people. Hated seeming common or average. Morticia was a little droopy, she admitted that to herself at least. But didn't Morts take on aspects of their human's personality? And wasn't Celosia a little droopy? Not everyone had to be peppy. She walked in, closing the gate between herself and her neighbor.

"See? Look at that. She's browning," her neighbor declared, pointing.

"She's never been the most green or canopied Mort."

Her neighbor shook her finger. "If you don't start taking better care of that Mort, I'm going to report a case of concern. For your own good."

In retrospect, Celosia wonders if her neighbor was actually legitimately concerned about her. But at the time, she responded like it was the attack she perceived it to be. "You know what would be really great?" she opened Morticia's door, "If you minded your own business." She tossed her bag onto the passenger seat, then climbed in. Morticia closed her own door and started to roll her vines toward the exit. The gate moved out of their way, and they were off. Celosia ignored the tell-tale creaking coming from Morticia. She was fine. It was fine. They were both fine.

She left Morticia in the long-term care solarium at the spaceport. She flew to her childhood planet. The bereavement officer tried to make a connection with her as they sat together in his office. She made the necessary grunts in response. Her father had had a heart attack. What more was there to say? But the officer leaned forward, sliding a piece of parchment to her. "I need you to sign this, stating that you understand that your father's heart attack's underlying cause was chronic alcoholism, and that it is a family disease. That if you see any of the early signs of it in yourself, you will seek help, as is your obligation for the good of our society."

Celosia stared at the parchment. Alcoholism? Her father was not an alcoholic. He enjoyed drinking the way foodies enjoyed food. He was quite posh about it, in fact. He knew what wine paired with what cheese. He had a special blender dedicated to mixed drinks. The worst you could say about him was he drank beer kind of like some people drank soda, but, really, it was light beer. She thought about protesting. But she'd protested official paperwork before in her life. It just ended up with time wasted and signing the document anyway. So she signed it. Who cared what the official paperwork said. She knew the truth about her father.

But then the bereavement officer let her into her father's flat. "So, just take what you want. Let us know when you're done. Our cleanup crew will come in and sort out what can be donated to society and what must . . ." he looked around the tight space, "be recycled or burned." He closed the door behind him with a slight snick.

It was a one-bedroom apartment. Probably nice at one point. Underneath all the piles. On the table. On the countertops. On the floor. They looked like piles of trash, but when she dug through one, she found a used book her father had bought at some point, still in the packaging. There were bags of empty cans and bottles. He had tried to clean it up, you could tell. But then there were also cans and bottles around the room. Worst of all, though, was in the bedroom. Lined up on the windowsill were multiple plant pots. Every single one with a dead plant in it. The last was a cactus. The cheapest kind you could get from the store. It was starting to shrivel but was still just barely alive. Celosia picked it up, sat among the clothes, paper, and dead leaves on her father's bed, and cried.

Celosia doesn't want to think about it anymore. Or what happened next. She tears herself out of the flashback and finds her face wet with tears, the Vibratium playing some sort of slow dirge. She stands up and backs away from the Solstera. Even though she doesn't want to think about it, the memories still come. How she took that cactus home with her, thinking she would be the one to save it. Only to get back to the long-term care solarium and discover that Morticia had been repossessed from her for neglect. Since she wouldn't admit to there being any sort of social, physical, or mental issue, she was banned from Mort ownership and relegated to bamboo bicycles. One of the few things left crafted from dead plants.

Now, here she is, a woman banned from owning any KreaturFreundin, responsible for a solarium full of them. Guilt tears at her heart like a vulture. Hazel wouldn't have left her with this task if she'd known the full story. She knows Celosia is in recovery. Knows that she had been deep in alcoholism's hole. But she's never told her about Morticia or the ruling. She's never told anybody.

A leaf brushes her shoulder, and she jumps away. A Saltatoria. Vines that dangle from the ceiling but sometimes move in a dance-like motion to a song if one is present in the room. She wonders who dances to a dirge, and the thought jars her enough that she scuttles out of the room, slamming the door behind her, then leaning against it. "You need to ground yourself," she orders. So she slides down to the floor and pushes her palms against it. In spite of the warmth of the door behind her, the tiles feel cool. That's sense number one. Touch.

She rapidly completes the five senses. Taste—metal in her mouth. Sight—the decorative hutch with a porcelain skeleton statuette drinking a cup of coffee displayed inside. Scent—a mix of smoke from the living room's fireplace and toast from Hazel's snack before she left. Hearing—the faint sound of the Vibratium on the other side of the door, playing the notes of a local sea shanty. This last is what does it for her. She laughs. And suddenly, she remembers not who she was, but who she is.

She is Celosia Larix. And one day, a week after her father died, as she rode her bicycle home from the liquor store, feeling the knowing stares of all the other adults on the street in their Morts, something inside her snapped. And she decided she would honor all the good aspects of her father by living up to them. Because she remembered the way one corner of his mouth lifted higher than the other when he smiled. And how his hands gently guided hers to stir cookie dough. And how reverently he handed her her first plant at the age of five, telling her, "Giving care to another living being is one of the greatest achievements for a human." How horrible that alcohol robbed him of that in the end.

So she parked her bicycle, went inside, and immediately dumped out all the liquor she had just bought. Then she went right back out to the local library and found books in the self-help section. Books about not drinking. She wasn't even sure what to call it at the time. She was embarrassed to check them out, so she read them in the library. Then she was sick in bed for the next three days. She knows now how dangerous it was to withdraw on her own.

Every day after that, she went to the library and read until it closed for the day. She didn't need to work for a while. Her father had left her a sizable inheritance thanks to his life insurance policy going solely to her. And that was lucky, for she was on the cusp of getting fired for tardiness and slovenliness anyway. She spent weeks reading in the library and sleeping all the times she wasn't there. And something started to shift in her.

She started to notice just how slovenly her own flat was. It honestly wasn't all that far behind her father's, now that she looked at it with sober eyes. So she started to clean it. And the act of cleaning it felt like it was scrubbing away something inside of her too. Leaving something raw and fresh and new. Or perhaps something unearthed from a long time ago.

That's when she stumbled upon it in the library: A book explaining that you freeze at the age at which your addiction to alcohol began. And you can only continue growing up when you stop. Celosia thought about how she started to drink her last year of university and began to wonder, what would someone about to graduate from university do? The thought struck her one morning as she locked her bike up at the bike rack next to all the children's bikes. The year before she started drinking, she'd talked a lot about traveling to another planet with a different ecosystem. She'd so enjoyed the difference of Viaria when she arrived from her childhood planet for university. But what had she actually done? Stayed right in the same place and stagnated. So she started to research other planets. On the day she discovered Algrüsti, she had just suffered through another bike ride full of stares from every passing human with a Mort. She swore she even heard a huff of disdain from a Mort itself at one point. So she looked up if there was any planet where most people bicycled. And Algrüsti came up.

Celosia pushes her back against the door and squares her shoulders. She is not the Celosia who graduated and stayed on Visaria so the party could continue and proceeded to fail to take care of anyone, including herself. She's the Celosia who lost her father and got sober in his memory, then moved to an entirely new planet where she could get a fresh start. Part of a fresh start, of a chance to be a new person, is to rise to challenges. She's not a person who gives up and drinks the day and shame away. She's a person who tries. A person who a friend messages when her father is dying to entrust her entire unusual home and solarium to.

Celosia stands up, turns, opens the door, and walks into the solarium. The Vibratium pauses in its song as the Saltatoria extends a vine toward her. She closes the door and turns to the caretaking list, reading it carefully. She picks up a watering can, turns on the solarium's faucet, and fills it, then turns back to the room. As she walks purposefully toward the first plant that needs daily watering, the Vibratium begins to play a tune. The beginning notes of a folk song her father used to sing to her. She continues to water the plants but begins to cry. How did this KreaturFreundin know this song's meaning to her? When she hasn't thought about it herself in years? When the last verse comes up, she sings along.

For my babe shall grow to a tall-reaching tree;

And even though crooked she may be,

I'll still be proud of her crown in the air,

Persisting through winds, storms, and despair.

The Vibratium sends out the final two notes as a lilting backdrop to her fading hold of the final word. Then, unusually for a KreaturFreundin that thrives on responding to human emotions, it falls into silence. The Saltatoria drapes a vine over her shoulder, and she reaches a hand up, stroking the soft, fuzzy leaves with her index finger.

THE WILLOW MAIDEN
∽ BEATRICE TOOTHMAN ∽

She ran as fast as her feet would carry her, soles sticking to the soft carpet of moss crawling across the forest floor, toes catching like velcro over every ragged and twisting root reaching toward the dimming light in the sky. She would be too late, she knew that already. The spoiled prince had said as much, but she had to see with her own eyes what she had begun to feel deep in her heart. She tripped once more over a fallen branch and scraped her wooden legs against the splintered debris of it, sprawling rather than landing and letting her forehead rest against the ground while she fought back tears. She could feel the warmth of the forest floor draining away from her as she raised her eyes to gaze upon her own destruction.

Her tree, a beautiful willow, once lush and green with languidly dripping leaves and delicately bent branches, was laying in shattered pieces on the ground. He had told her he would do it. Told her he would rather see her destroyed than be without her. But part of her had hoped it was only passion talking, for men do and say strange things when they're in love. At least, that's what the other Willow Maidens had told her, and Ash and Rowan had seconded their claims. As she staggered towards the ruin of her body, she did not think she could bring herself to believe that this was what love was capable of.

Only the stump with what was left of her roots was left intact by the Prince's cruel destruction. Roots she had dug deep into the earth for decades, forging her own pathways with thousands of tiny decisions every day on which avenues through the rich soil would best lead to her continued growth and well-being. And soon that would be gone, decaying into the earth and leaving nothing but a rotten memory. Her bruised and battered body began to stiffen. Just as her tree would return its essence to the forest floor, so too would her body.

A flock of starlings shot overhead as a whirring, clicking noise approached from somewhere down the man-made path to her left. Her heart quaked. She had thought the path a blessing at first; how lucky she was to have sprouted so close to the path her human lover would wander down on his wheeled beast. She had thought him handsome, with his jet-black hair and regal posture; she had even mistaken his sneer for a smile. Every visit ended with his proclamations of love and ardor, begging her to come home with him and be his forever. She tried to explain as gently as she could that she loved him passionately, but she belonged to the forest. To leave her canopied home for him would be akin to inviting death on their honeymoon journey; for she could not live without her tree, nor it without her.

He had tried to take her by force yesterday, dragging her ruthlessly through brambles and berry thickets who were doing their best to cling to her with their frail and spindly branches in order to keep her within the forests' boundaries. He had bound her hands and legs and tied her to the small metal shelf above his back wheel, but he had done the job haphazardly, and she was able to thrust her fingers into the spinning spokes. Her hand had splintered terribly, the fingers shattered and aching, but it had been enough to bring the mechanical beast to a sudden stop, sending the prince flying across the handlebars and onto the smooth dirt of the path. Her sister Oak had moved quickly, snapping exposed roots across the path to scoop her bound body into the cavernous safety of the root system below. For what seemed like hours as her fingers healed and grew in the protection of the loamy soil, she listened to the man she loved beg for her forgiveness. His cries were solemn and regretful, at first, but soon they grew desperate and rageful. He cursed her name and the names of her sisters, claiming that they were temptresses and demonesses who lured men's hearts only to let them wither like rotten fruit upon their spent branches. He lamented his actions in the same breath he promised her execution. And then he was gone, pedaling his broken beast down the same path they had walked as lovers just yesterday. She had stayed with Oak, out of fear and necessity, until the next afternoon when a cold shock of pain and nausea had wracked her wooden body so hard she thought she was going to dissolve into pieces at her sister's feet. It was then that she knew the Prince had made good on his promise, just as surely as she knew now that it was his wheeled beast whirring and clicking down the darkening path towards her to finish the job.

But as she gazed down the path, expecting her end, she saw a different beast hauling a cart behind it with another rider altogether perched on its back. The woman pedaled backward to bring the beast to a stop, eyes wide as she took in the scene before her. The Willow Maiden, shedding dying bark and sap-tinged tears into the earth, stared back. "What happened to you?" the woman asked, removing the hard, acorn-shaped helmet encasing her head and revealing vibrant shorn hair the color of holly berries. "Are you hurt? Do you need help?" She leaned her beast against Ash, who promptly tried to shove it to the ground; the cart was heavy enough to keep the beast upright, but only just. The woman didn't even seem to notice as she carefully stepped around the scattered detritus of branches and leaves toward the Willow Maiden. She stopped just shy of reaching out to her and crouched down on her boot-clad feet instead.

"I am dying," the Willow Maiden whispered, "He has killed me with his love, just as he promised he would do."

The woman frowned, "Love didn't do this. But I think I can help you if you want me to try." She extended her hand towards the Willow Maiden and smiled gently. "My name is Hayley."

The Willow Maiden did not want to return to the earth. Not yet. Not when the sun was dappling the forest floor with the shadows of her sister's leaves. Not when the wind blew so gently across the Maiden's cheek to harden the sticky tears that spilled down her chin. Not when she wanted to see so much more, to be so much more than the ruined husk the prince had left in his wake.

This woman, Hayley, had a smudge of dirt on her cheek, and her brilliant hair was stuck to her forehead with sweat, looking for all the world like a cockscomb in spring. Her mechanical beast looked old and had orange spots of rust along its body resembling flowers in bloom. Hayley was rooted to the earth as surely as the Willow Maiden, albeit in a different way, that much was clear. She tentatively reached out her hand, healed from yesterday's trauma but now flaking to pieces on the ground. "I am a Willow Maiden," she rasped.

Hayley gingerly reached towards the Maiden's hand but, seeing the falling pieces flutter in the breeze, thought better of it and offered a sad smile instead. "Hold on just a second, Willow, I'll be right back—I promise." She didn't have the strength to correct Hayley on her name; her limbs were growing weaker as she sagged further into the ground. A rummaging sound, then a metallic clang sounded from Hayley's wheeled beast, and a moment later she stood in front of the Maiden with a large bucket full of sloshing liquid. "I think if we can get you in here, it will at least slow down what's happening to your body. You know . . . like putting budding branches that fall on the ground into water so the buds can still open."

The Maiden thought on this for a moment before nodding, slowly. "I don't think I can," she wheezed, her voice diminishing in size, just like her body, as she shrank and began to sink into the forest floor.

"Can I pick you up to help? Is that okay?" The Willow Maiden nodded, almost imperceptible this time, as her strength was reaching its end.

And then she was being lifted, carefully, Hayley's arms solid and gentle underneath her own as she guided the Willow Maiden into the cool relief of the bucket. Ice-cold water flowed over the sides, and for the first time in hours, the Maiden was able to draw a full, albeit shaky breath as the water penetrated her skin and began coursing underneath her bark to fill the hollow spaces that had formed within her. "Is that okay? Are you okay?" Hayley was crouched at eye level and peered at the Maiden anxiously.

"Yes." She sighed, relief plumping the dried bark of her throat. Something in her face must have reassured Hayley, because she smiled and breathed her own sigh of relief before grabbing both sides of the bucket and standing, being careful not to jostle the water or Maiden, and then walking over to her beast and gently placing Maiden and bucket in the wheeled cart tied to its rear. Cords were swiftly arranged around the bucket to prevent further disturbance to its contents, and Hayley managed a quick "I'll be right back!" before dashing to the corpse of the Maiden's tree. The Maiden heard twigs snapping and limbs being gingerly rolled across the ground, but was too exhausted to bring herself to open her eyes. Relishing instead the warmth of the sun on her swelling bark, and the relieved sounds of her sister's leaves rustling and swaying as they spoke to each other.

She was awakened sometime later by the sound of people talking, small children playing, and chickens rustling and squawking as they darted out of the way of Hayley's beast. "I thought you were going to get water from the well," a voice spoke from close by. "What happened?" The Maiden opened her eyes sluggishly and saw another woman standing next to Hayley and peering into the cart with concern.

"Well, I got the water, but . . ." Hayley let the sentence trail off and reached for the bucket. "How are you feeling?" she asked as she carefully plodded towards the open door of a small thatched cottage.

"I'm not sure," the Maiden said, voice stronger than before, "Better, I think." The woman who had spoken to Hayley moved into view as she crouched down to clear a space on the floor next to several wheeled beasts in various states of deconstruction. Wheels shone brightly in the light from the fire burning in the back wall of the cluttered space. The woman kicked a few more tools out of the way, and, seemingly satisfied, addressed the Maiden directly.

"Who did this to you, Love?"

"Willow, her name is Willow," Hayley commented over her shoulder as she shuffled back out of the door from which she had come.

"Okay, Willow, what happened?" She was tall, much taller than Hayley, with skin the color of hazelnuts and a torso that was thick and sturdy like Sister Oak's.

"The prince, he loved me, and I would not go with him. I could not. . . ." The Maiden shuddered, the water suddenly feeling as cold as ice as she recalled the rage in the prince's eyes.

"That's okay, Willow. . . . Love, I understand." She blew an errant glossy curl off of her forehead with more force than was necessary.

Hayley returned, carrying a thick bundle of the Maiden's tree, shattered ends looking like severed limbs, twigs snapping dryly even as she carefully settled the bundle onto the floor of the cottage away from the fire. "Gretchen, I thought maybe," Hayley rubbed a hand through her hair, making it stand straight up and look even more birdlike than before, "Maybe if we can preserve the wood. Maybe we can, I dunno." Hayley sighed, looking slightly defeated, as if this was a better idea in the dim light of the forest and perhaps not such a good one in the bright light of the cottage.

The firelight caught in Gretchen's eye as she considered the pile of wood for a moment, scratching her chin with her forefinger and thumb. The gleam turned to a spark, and an understanding of Hayley's idea lit up her face from within. "Well, why not? It's worth a try, isn't it?" Gretchen turned to the Willow Maiden. "Willow, we're going to try something, but I want you to know that it might not work. You might still die, and it's going to take a few days. I don't know how long you're going to last in that bucket."

The Maiden considered this. These women were nothing like her Prince. They were kind. They asked her things before doing them. They were trying to help her for her sake, not because of anything they thought they could get from her. "I will try to hold on. The water is cold. My body will last," she looked up at Hayley, "as long as the buds of spring."

Hayley grinned and turned to Gretchen, "We have to try."

Days passed in the little cottage. The Maiden only knew that much because Hayley and Gretchen slept for some hours on the little stuffed mattress stashed in the corner. The rest of the cottage was taken up by mechanical beasts and their parts. She had learned the human word for them on the second day shortly after Hayley came to put the Maiden in a new bucket with fresh water. "We make *bicycles* for this village and the one next to us." She had smiled at the Maiden's use of both mechanical and wheeled beasts instead of the proper term, but she didn't laugh at her, not like the prince would have. "I could see how you would come up with that as a term for my bicycles, though," Gretchen had called over from where she was sanding and oiling a few of the Maiden's tree limbs. "I make 'em tough and sturdy. There's no room for a whole lot else away from the Castle and its paved roads."

More days passed, Hayley and Gretchen talking with the Maiden as they worked. She watched in wonder as they sanded and oiled and shaped her old tree into something wondrous and new. Light streaming in from the cottage windows danced along the grain of a carefully molded seat, then a gently curved handlebar. The Maiden was fascinated, sitting in her little bucket. For the first couple of days she had remained small and weary, a diminished version of the beautiful and mighty thing she had once been. But each day as she talked with Hayley and Gretchen, learned about the village and its neighbors, and was spoken to like she was a welcome part of it all and not an outsider resource to be claimed, she began to grow. Her voice was stronger, her wooden heart beat with the tentative pull of hope, and her limbs spilled over the sides of the bucket until she was almost bigger than she was before she met the Prince. With only her rear end firmly planted in the bucket now, her wooden toes tapped an optimistic rhythm against the bare floor of the cottage as she watched her tree finish its transformation into something new and wondrous under Gretchen and Hayley's skillful hands.

Gretchen held the finished bicycle by its handlebars. The wood seemed to glow from within, and as Hayley held out her hand to help the Maiden stand, her heart stuttered in recognition. The nearly empty bucket rolled behind her, and she carefully took one step, then two, Hayley offering her forearms for support as she walked backward with the Maiden toward where Gretchen was waiting. The Maiden reached out a tentative hand and lightly stroked the polished surface of the saddle. The wood warmed under her fingers, and the glow of the bicycle intensified, visibly pulsating to the same rhythm of the Maiden's own heart as it recognized its former home, transformed into something new.

Gretchen and Hayley stared, open-mouthed as the light finally began to dim, leaving the room bathed in the afterglow. "Well, I think it worked!" Hayley was the first to speak, giggling and giddy as she did so.

"Will it continue to work is the question." Gretchen said, worrying her bottom lip with her teeth, concern furrowing her brow. "The water has worked so far, but without roots . . ." She stopped, gazing at the Maiden in wonder as she tenderly stroked the glossy wood of the bicycle's handlebars. First one bud, then another, began to grow and bloom from the surface of the luminescent wood beneath the Maiden's gentle touch.

"There is more than one way to connect to the earth beneath your feet," the Maiden smiled at the new growth reaching towards the bright afternoon sunshine. "As long as I have the sun and the rain . . ." She closed her eyes and pressed her hand over her heart, feeling the growing threads of connection between herself, her bicycle, and the soil beneath them both weave new pathways through the soft bark of her skin to the very core of her heart. It felt like home.

"What do you think, do you wanna take her on a test ride?" Gretchen asked, a satisfied grin spreading across her face. The Maiden sighed, a mixture of happiness and relief.

"I'd like that." She ran her hands along the seat with one hand and, releasing Hayley's arm, grasped the handlebar with the other.

"You don't have to come back if you don't want to," Gretchen said as the Maiden took her first tentative steps out of the cottage door, her tree rolling along at her side.

"But we'd like you to if you want. You're welcome here anytime," Hayley said as she walked over to put her arm around Gretchen's middle and pull her close.

The Maiden turned and smiled, "Thank you."

The sun was bright and warm as she walked out onto the dirt road that led out of the village. Vendors were setting up their stalls for the day while scrubby blue birds called out to each other from the trees nearest the forest path. An apple rolled to a stop in front of her wheel, and she bent down to pick it up and hand it to the round-faced woman who was trotting after it. The woman smiled as she stopped to huff and catch her breath, "Nah, love, you keep it, I got plenty for the day anyway. You travelin' through or new to town? If it's fruit and sundry items you're after, you just stop by my booth and I'll fix you up, right as rain!" The sentences came out of the cheerful woman in such a rush as she wiped her hands on her apron that they almost sounded like one long word.

The Maiden rolled the apple in her hand and smiled, feeling the warm earth under her feet and the solid comfort of her tree with its sturdy wheels and glossy pedals. She took a bite of the apple, savoring the tartness and juicy sweetness. It tasted like the beginning of a new season. It tasted like freedom. "I am new. My name is Willow."

OAKS, SPOKES, OUR FOLKS
∽ KELLEY TAI ∾

Kalix thought I was out of my mind when I handed her the invitation to my bachelorette party.

"You're lost in zero gravity," she said. "*I'm* the maid of honor here."

I had snuck into her room—our previous room—after work when she was still at the lab. Kalix never bothered changing the keycode, and now I guess she never would.

It was strange seeing the room half-lived. Cardboard boxes stacked on top of each other, Kalix's thrifted blazers and faded plaid skirts flung across the carpet like she was putting together outfits for her first day of school (she probably was). I spotted the notebooks we found in the garbage room last week—thick sheets of college-ruled paper, unwritten and untouched—tucked away in her faded gray backpack.

I didn't give Kalix a chance to change. She was still in her lab coat when I handed her the pink envelope.

And that's when Kalix started complaining.

I ignored her and climbed to my old top bunk, resuming the game of poker on my phone. Like all sleeping quarters on *Turtle*, during this rendered evening, the lights behind the beds illuminated a blue hue, so our circadian cycles matched a supposed night, though I had never been planet-side long enough to know what that really meant.

If Mama has the energy for it, maybe I'll find out on Gesneriana. *I had imagined one too many times the sounds of the cicadas playing a waltz as I walked down the aisle, Wildner and I faded against a pink sunset glow.* I'd be holding a bouquet of mirias, bioluminescent flowers natively grown on Gesneriana. Maybe, *hopefully*, we would get to see them too.

"This wasn't supposed to happen," Kalix murmured, pacing back and forth. "I love you, Winter, but I can't accept. I won't."

When you were born in the same space cruiser, bundled together as the only two kids in the same grade with the same birthday month, nearly sharing the same last name, it was hard not to be someone's best friend. It was harder to wait for them to get over themselves.

"Are you done?" I rolled my eyes. "I want to go home."

Kalix pointed the invitation up at me like I was to blame for fun existing. "I told you I'd throw you something small, you didn't have to—"

"It's *fine*." I snatched the invitation and stuffed it underneath a pillow. "You and my mom are coming with me. End of story."

"But—"

"No buts."

"But I can't use your money—"

"You can, and now you can practice biking before going to Cana*duh*." I climbed down the bunk and sat on her bed. "I want you to save up. Don't feel guilty, please."

Kalix studied her brains off to get into McGill, and living on Earth was stupid expensive—especially with the yearly increase of the planet-side home tax—but Kalix was going to make a difference, I knew it. She was going to make Earth better again for all of us, and since she was going to miss the wedding at the Gesneriana Gardens, this was the least I could do. I didn't care who hosted anyway. I just wanted us to be together for one last time. Before she moved, before Mama—

I pictured the three of us, side by side, on a path, Gesneriana oak peaches in each of our hands. I read somewhere that 1 percent of the planet's entire economy came from these peaches. Another 0.5 percent came from the export of mirias.

Kalix sank into the bed next to me. "I'm sorry for being dramatic. Of course, I'll be there. Thank you. I—" she paused "—I don't deserve you."

I jumped from the bed before we both started crying. "Just do me a favor. Don't go touching random things, especially the miria flowers. They stain."

"But I love touching things." Kalix held on to my hand. "It's the scientist in me."

"And, don't forget we get access to the fireworks at night. Bring your—"

Kalix grabbed the little rubber cones from her nightstand. "Earplugs. For my sensitive hearing, yeah, yeah. I got it."

And I got *them*—Kalix, me, and Mama. On Gesneriana. Rhyming, as poetry does.

∽ · ∾

"Put your legs on the two pedals here," Hansa said. The owner of the rental store also doubled as a marathon cyclist during the weekend, prompting Kalix to conspicuously check out their calves after finding out. "You need to start pedaling first, Winter, and then your mom will catch on. Don't worry, most folks balance out in the end. Any questions?"

The bike was as conventional as a bike could be. A black frame, with a woven basket at the front. But I was barely able to walk in a straight line with this chunky helmet on, and the image of myself wobbling on a bike made me laugh.

"How do I stop the straps from scratching my chin?" Hansa chuckled. "Just so you know, if it ends up with only you biking, you can turn on the battery here. It'll activate the cycle assist."

Mama sat behind me in the two-seater. She didn't understand Plain English anyway, so she sat there behind me, absentminded, staring at the butterflies. *Butterflies*. They looked like little angels, wings attached to the millipedes we see crawling behind water filtration tanks.

I turned around with a grin. "Māmā nǐ hái hǎo ma?" *How are you doing Mama?*

At first, she looked at me with glassy eyes, and all I could hear was the doctor in my head. *Early signs of dementia include being confused about time and place.*

"Hái hǎo ma?" I asked again, giving her a thumbs up.

She signed back with a glint in her eyes.

I gave her a small smile. She was going to be fine.

And there was Kalix, jumping up and down with her camera pointed toward us. Gravity on Gesneriana was much less than on *Turtle*, and Kalix must have been at least a foot up in the air. "I can see the end of the world!"

"Don't break your ankle," I told her.

"Don't get your dress dirty," she sang.

I thought it was fitting to wear a white sundress, but . . . she was right. I hadn't considered what it meant to be outside, but perhaps that's what made being planet-side so much more captivating to me. It wasn't controlled, a kind of wild I'd only find outside a space cruiser.

"*I'm kidding*," Kalix said. "You're beautiful no matter what. Come on, I've been recording this whole time."

Mama already had one leg on the back pedal. Maybe she was remembering and not only copying me. She used to tell me that biking was the best part of living on Earth.

I took a breath, focused on the wheels and the gravel path, and pushed the pedals. Something spun underneath me, a mechanical clicking sound.

"The spokes," Hansa said, when they noticed I was looking down.

Mama and I couldn't find a groove at first, but then we were moving—very slowly, an inch, and then five, and then the wheels underneath me were spinning. It was a strange, almost surreal feeling of balancing on a bike, using my legs to push the pedals, to turn the wheels, to move the bike forward, with the soft ticking of the spokes underneath me and Mama behind me.

I breathed out a sound, a gasp or laughter, up to the sky, to *Turtle*, to Wildner, while Kalix snapped photos of us biking in circles.

∽ • ∾

It shouldn't be possible for the Gardens to be even larger than our space cruiser, but the Gesneriana Gardens stretched out for hundreds of miles like it was its own country.

We took the biking trail easiest for beginners—at least that's what Hansa had told us earlier—but the rolling hills were nothing like the "mountain" simulations we did in spin class. I gripped the handlebars tighter as we climbed uphill. I thought Mama was out of breath too, but she didn't say anything. We were silent, pushing down on pedals that didn't want to be pushed down, but I soon realized that uphills always paid off because Mama was always excited to go down, where we went fast, and then faster. The wind rushed around my ears. I strained hard, listening, in case it was telling me a secret. Kalix had her eyes closed, arms out to the sides.

Our tickets for the bike tour included a lunch, and of course I'd paid extra for peach picking.

We parked our bikes by a river that cut through a quarter of the way into the Gardens, and then entered the private orchard.

Hundreds of the Gesneriana oaks were cultivated in rows, and, in the oak trees, on top of a bough, peaches twinkled under the sunlight, like special power-ups from video game simulations.

"How many do we get to pick, again?" Kalix asked with her mouth full. She had inhaled her chicken sandwich.

"One ticket, one peach," I said, helping Mama break her lunch into bite-sized chunks. "But any more is weighed. It's like two hundred dollars per pound or something."

Kalix nodded quickly, "Just one then."

A bit later, she screamed from the oak trees, "But *which* one?"

I hopped over past the picnic tables and understood why Kalix was flustered. Somehow these real-life peaches were as *unreal* as the simulations. Golden-orange and fuzzy, they sat on the trees like art decorations. I felt like they were not meant to be disturbed, picked at, prodded.

But nature, Wildner always said, was a process, not a thing.

The peach ripped off the stem easily in a sharp crunch.

It felt so *right* in my hands, a peach that was equally firm as it was plump and heavy. I imagined the insides filled with juice.

I hurried and picked another one, closer to the edge of the river. The peaches here were dewy, gently coated with fresh water, and I loved that it was touched by another part of Gesneriana.

"You picked two already?" Kalix cried when I walked by.

She was still empty-handed.

"You snooze, you lose."

"Wait, wait. Don't eat them without me!"

∾ • ∾

When the Gesneriana Gardeners took away my two tickets—one from Mama, one from me—I thought I would feel grief, a death in a dream, but my world felt lighter. Everything was going exactly as I had imagined.

I skipped over to Mama; I think she was more excited than me. She grabbed one of the peaches before I could even sit down. Mama's demeanor changed, then. Someone who lived in black and white suddenly seeing the world in color again.

"Děng yī xià," I said. *Wait.* "Wǒ hái méi bāng nǐ xiāo pí." I hadn't even started peeling the fruit for her yet.

But Mama bit through the skin with no problem.

"Hǎo chī," she cried. "**好吃, 好吃**."

Tastes good.

She almost did a little dance as she munched, her eyes closed, a smile on her face. I wondered what Baba would say if he could see her now.

Kalix came back, out of breath, holding a peach twice as big as mine and Mama's.

"What the hell is that?" I asked. "Where did you find it?"

"When you snooze," Kalix said, squeezing beside me. "You find a better peach."

"That doesn't . . . sound good."

"Whatever. Are you ready?"

We clanked our peaches together.

When I finally took a bite—I sighed inwardly, outwardly. I'd never had anything so sweet, this fresh and luscious before. The peach was spring inside my mouth, refreshing after a morning of biking. Like an advertisement, I was tasting the sun. Juice ran down my lips, but I didn't care as I slobbered it back up. Kalix laughed at me, but then peach juice also started spilling down her lips, and we cackled and cackled until tears smudged our mascaras.

I wanted to bow down to the Gardens. *Thank you, thank you, for this fruit.*

Wildner was going to love it here. I could easily see us reading our vows underneath these oak trees, feeding each other peaches instead of cake.

~ • ~

We biked through the Gardens until the sky burned a faint orange and pink.

It was my first sunset. So many firsts for a day: first time being planet-side, first time picking peaches, first time watching a sunset. I was ready to take on more firsts, but Mama had stopped biking with me, and her words disappeared into signs again.

"We should go after the fireworks," I said to Kalix in between breaths. We were already on our way to the amphitheater. "I'm also super hungry."

Kalix looked at Mama and nodded. "I guess we won't see the miria after all."

"Maybe you can glow in the dark for me instead," I joked.

There was no direct trail, and the rumbles from the uneven garden floor tickled *up up up* in my hands. With the cycle assist, I felt even more grateful for the bicycle, hard at work. Only a bike gave me the opportunity to weave in between trees, pedal with the wild rabbits running by our side.

You made everything come true, I told the bicycle and caressed the frame when no one was watching.

By the time we got to the amphitheater, the stars filled up the night. There were always stars in space—they were another cliché, an invisible thing to us—but on Gesneriana, the stars meant something different. It signaled change, a turn. Maybe *this* was what night meant. Nighttime was like a wallflower hanging behind the sun, a secret admirer holding a bouquet underneath the moonlight.

Crowds of families walked with us into the amphitheater, and I realized I had never been anywhere with a swarm of people before. My chest tightened. Was this how Mama felt before leaving Earth, constantly pressed up against hundreds of unfamiliar faces? Kalix didn't seem to mind the rush of people though. She looked like she wanted to hug everyone and ask questions about where they came from, in typical Kalix fashion.

I focused on the rhythm of the spokes and breathed in and out. *Click, click, click.* And just like that, the sound blurred out the crowd around me.

"Winter, look," Kalix said suddenly. "Is that—is that what I think it is?"

It was easy to spot the flowers. The miria blossoms were bright yellow and green, twinkling like the stars above us. Glow-in-the-dark, exactly as promised; it was no wonder moths were drawn to flames. For a moment, I felt like I was surrounded by space again, and only the petal's light was guiding us towards flowers and land.

"Māmā," I tapped her gently. "Nǐ kàn." *Look.*

Mama clapped her hands together.

A steep set of stairs led down to the amphitheater, but we settled on the lawn instead, where we could see the flowers. As we laid down our bikes, the spokes were still spinning, and I was grateful for their familiar lullaby.

The three of us took photos with the miria in all kinds of iterations. Me in the middle, Mama and Kalix on the side. Mama and me. Kalix and me, with Mama taking the photos. Kalix and me, taking selfies.

And then, while Kalix was showing me the pictures, I don't know what came over me, maybe I shouldn't have touched them, but I made sure to be careful, brushing my hands against the petals that felt like velvet in my fingers. The flowers seemed to move toward me like they wanted to hold my hand too.

"Look at you and your mom," Kalix said softly, angling the picture towards me.

I replied by smearing my hands all over her face.

"What the hell," Kalix cried, touching her face. A couple wearing matching sweaters and baseball caps looked over.

The next thing I knew, I tasted Kalix's powdered fingers in my mouth.

"Take that, you shit!" She cackled.

I squealed and launched another counterattack on her collarbones.

I forgot where I was, how I was supposed to act—could I get kicked out of my wedding venue? But no one stopped us.

We were both out of breath in a brief SOS when Mama pointed at me, giggling, "Nǐ de qún zi."

Kalix's mouth dropped open. "Oh shit."

My dress was smudged with soot and soil, turning the white into a dusty gray. The bottom was torn, and the lace detail ripped to delicate threads. I was, at the same time, my own stepsister and Cinderella, but I would have shown up to the ball for Prince Charming, for Wildner, like this anyway.

When the fireworks went off, I couldn't be bothered watching them. It was Mama and Kalix I wanted to see all the time. I wanted so badly to take this moment back to *Turtle*—a present where I didn't need to worry about the next health appointment, how often Kalix and I were going to see each other. But the fireworks didn't stop, and time wouldn't either.

I held both their hands, now brushed with flower dust, and hoped the stain would never wash off.

WHEELS OF PROGRESS
℘ LISA TIMPF ℘

Avery Mackey coasted beside the field, dividing her attention between the GPS unit mounted on the handlebars and the dusty farm lane. She stopped and leaned her bike against one of the posts set around the fields for that purpose, then took a cross-path through the carrot patch, stopping when she reached the defective sensor.

She saw no visible reason why the device had stopped sending readings to the master computer. She'd have to take it apart at the workbench to diagnose the problem.

After grabbing a replacement sensor from her pack, Avery replaced the failed unit. She calibrated the new sensor, then hurried back to her bike.

Before remounting, she pulled her cell phone out of its holster and toggled the screen, taking the master AI program off standby mode. Based on moisture content data from the sensors, the AI program triggered the irrigation system. Long arcs of water spurted over several sectors of the field, including the one she'd just left.

Avery sighed as she swung up onto her bike and pedaled toward the farm's workshop.

That's three sensors I had to replace today. I'll have to fab up more. She'd hoped for some free time this afternoon. Between online classes, training for the bike race, and completing her field chores, she'd had precious little of that, lately.

Technology is supposed to save time, Avery thought. *It will, once I figure out why the sensors keep failing.*

ᦓ · ᦓ

Avery slid the window above the workbench open so she could continue to enjoy the fresh air. Usually, when she toiled here, Avery did so comforted by the memories of all the pleasant times she'd spent chatting with her father. He'd been a paramedic by trade, but also enjoyed working with his hands, so, during his off hours, he spent a lot of time in this very workshop.

Today, preoccupied by other thoughts, Avery couldn't summon his image. She'd only been twelve when he'd died during a particularly bad round of viral infections. As the years had passed, it became more and more difficult to hang on to the memories.

"More failed sensors?"

Recognizing her mother's voice, Avery turned. She saw Claire Mackey run a hand across her forehead, leaving a smear of grease. "Looks like you've got problems of your own."

Claire glanced at her hands and nodded. "The van's been acting up."

"The sensors, too. I used my last replacement today. And I don't have materials to fab up more than a dozen or so. It's frustrating, the way they keep giving out."

"We need to design better sensors. Ones that don't fail." Claire put a hand on her daughter's shoulder. "When you go to Toronto Tech, you'll learn how."

"I haven't confirmed my spot yet."

"That'll come. At next year's Fair."

∾ · ∾

When she swung up on her speed bike later that afternoon, Avery considered her mother's parting words. With her day's work complete, the time for play had come. A serious kind of play, because her performance in the bike races would have a bearing on her future.

Avery pedaled toward the team's rendezvous point for today's ride, thinking about the Fair.

Because of the ongoing rounds of viral illnesses that continued to circle the globe, inhabitants of towns and cities across Canada usually kept their distance and minimized contact with members of other communities, going masked when necessary. In April and October, semi-annual vaccines targeted at the most prevalent variants allowed for the broadening of social circles. Waning immunity generally dictated a return to greater isolation after two months of freedom.

The Fair, the fall gathering in Avery's region, took place in mid-October. A longtime tradition, it dated back to 1840. Once, the event had consisted of midway rides, agricultural displays, and horse shows. Now, like its counterparts across the country, the Fair also hosted sporting competitions, including bike races. It was at these that Avery hoped to make her mark.

Larger universities throughout North America still offered varsity sports, with athletes receiving extra booster shots to reduce the risk of cross infection. After Hollywood's collapse, sports, including those played at universities, had become an even bigger draw than in the past. University scouts prowled the grandstands at the county fairs across the country, hoping to sign talented athletes. Earning a scholarship would be Avery's ticket out of the village of Windham, at least for a while.

This year's two-hour bike relay wasn't the big one for Avery and her friends. All four members of Avery's team had another year of high school to complete after this one. Still, it would serve as a practice run for the real thing, and a chance to attract the attention of scouts.

Having reached the crest of the hill that Gina had set as the meeting point, Avery halted. She'd arrived early, as usual. With time on her hands, she glanced at the valley below. Her eyes widened.

The nearest fields had some neat rows, but there were also clumps and clusters. Yellow and red flowers bloomed among the vegetables. Poles hammered into the ground supported corn as well as something else she couldn't discern. A woman wandered through the foliage, sometimes reaching down to pick up a handful of soil or move a leaf aside to check for pests.

She could be doing all of that remotely. I wonder why she isn't?

The whir of approaching tires signaled the arrival of Avery's teammates.

She followed her friends along the roadway, pondering the mystery of the field below.

Then she shrugged. Not everyone was a fan of progress. Perhaps it was as simple as that.

∽ • ∾

As she coasted toward the farm after the ride, Avery smiled. Gina had set up a good run, not too taxing this close to the big race but enough to give everyone's legs and lungs a decent workout.

Avery rode toward the workshop to store her bike for the night. As she approached the building, she stopped abruptly. A luxury vehicle, black with chrome trim, sat in front of the building. And from the workshop itself—

That's Mom's voice. And she's arguing with someone—

Reluctant to intrude, Avery dismounted and slipped around to the side of the building. She grimaced. She hadn't closed the window above the workbench. As a result of that open portal, she could hear the conversation clearly.

Avery glanced around. She didn't dare progress further, in case she might be seen through the window, or heard if she stepped on some loose gravel. Like it or not, it seemed her best option was to stay put.

"I'm not going to sell, and that's final." Her mother's voice, again.

Sell? Sell what?

"Maybe not now, but I'm sure you'll come to your senses. I understand you still have an outstanding balance on your loan . . ." A man's voice Avery didn't recognize offered a rebuttal to Claire's remarks.

"We have until next November to pay it off," Claire protested.

"But if it's not cleared by that time . . . I understand the banks are reluctant, these days, to extend credit for ventures such as yours, given the economic climate."

If Claire Mackey opted to respond to that comment, Avery couldn't discern what she said.

"Just remember, there's no guarantee my offer will remain as generous if you wait."

"I'll make a note of that," Claire said, in a tone Avery knew only too well.

Avery stayed put until the rumble of the car's engine faded into the distance. She bit her lower lip. Had her mother left, as well?

There was one way to find out.

Avery rolled her bike into the workshop.

"Did you hear any of that?" Claire Mackey's voice froze Avery for a moment.

"I didn't mean to." Avery parked her bike, then turned to her mother. "Who *was* that?"

"Malvin Annson. He's on the Council, but he's also got a lot of influence."

"Money, you mean." Avery didn't attempt to hide the bitterness in her tone.

"That, too. He made an offer on the farm. Based on what he's done in other counties, I imagine he plans to use it for a housing development."

"There's lots of vacant houses! Why build more?"

Claire sighed. "Because some people who can afford it would rather buy new."

"Why's he so set on *our* farm?"

"I'm sure you can guess."

Avery walked over to close the window and took in the view, feeling a pang as she did so. "It's one of the most beautiful spots in the county."

"Yes."

Avery stared, unseeing, at the fields for a moment. Did she really want to know the answer to the next question?

She had to ask.

"You said you weren't going to sell. Did you mean it?"

"The farm's been in our family for over a century. I'll hold out as long as I can." Claire's voice softened. "But there's your future to think about. Selling the farm would guarantee we'd have the money to pay for tuition, even if you don't land a sports scholarship."

Avery hesitated. What *about* her dreams of attending university? About getting away from here?

Suddenly those didn't seem as important as keeping the farm. "Don't worry about me. We'll figure it out," she said, hoping her tone conveyed greater conviction than she felt.

∽ • ∾

On Opening Day, Avery completed her farm tasks quickly, then rode out to the fairgrounds on Windham's western edge. Though she'd arranged to meet her friends at the midway, Avery's first stop was the Agricultural Building. She wanted to know how the farm's entries had fared in the vegetable competitions.

Steeling herself for disappointment—there had, after all, been challenges this year with the sensors—she checked out the displays, leaving the butternut squash for last. As she wandered through the exhibit hall, Avery felt alternate surges of elation and dismay.

Though the farm's vegetables had garnered third and fourth spot in many categories, and the butternut squash earned a second-place finish, one name kept popping up on the specimens tagged with first-place ribbons.

Sunset Valley Farms.

I wonder who that is?

At the end of an aisle, Avery reached a broad open area where a number of exhibitors had set up booths. Even their own farm had a display, which, Avery noted, was currently staffed by her mother. A man in a blue jacket with a FreshItUp logo stood conversing with Claire.

Good. Looks like there's some interest in our produce.

Avery studied the other booths. Most of the farms were promoting the products they were most known for. The booth at the end of the hall had a different kind of display, photo-boards of fields and close-ups of plants. One of the photos looked teasingly familiar.

Avery walked over for a closer look. She spotted a trophy at the back of the booth and shot a look at the banner hanging above it. *Sunset Valley Farms*, the banner proclaimed in large block letters. Below, in smaller type, was written, *Madelaine Stone*. Beside the name was a photo.

Avery glanced at the photo on the banner, then at the woman behind the booth's counter. *Must be Madelaine Stone. Unless she has a twin.*

She returned her attention to the display board. "Was this picture taken in the field you can see from Ridge Road?"

"It was," Madelaine said.

"Why the flowers? And the—" *Strange wouldn't be the right word. But what?* "Choice of arrangement?"

"I do what's referred to as companion planting. Take this example." Madelaine pointed to the center photograph. "Corn, climbing beans, and squash. The Haudenosaunee and other Indigenous peoples called this combination the Three Sisters. The corn provides a scaffold for the beans to climb. The beans fix nitrogen in the soil and help stabilize the corn. And the squash, with its broad leaves, helps keep moisture in the soil."

Madelaine waved at the board, broadly indicating other examples. "Basil, planted near tomatoes, repels harmful insects. Planting flowers alongside vegetables can attract pollinators, increasing yields."

"I've heard about companion planting," Avery said. She frowned. "There's some scientific backup, but I haven't seen a program yet that includes it."

The woman shot a glance toward the other farms' displays, then returned her attention to Avery. "You're Claire Mackey's daughter, aren't you?"

"Yes. You know my mother?"

"We went to high school together." Madelaine left it at that. "I've heard that you're on one of the bike teams. Do you ride using a program? Does a computer tell you when to speed up and when to slow down? When to conserve energy, and when to expend it?"

"No." Avery frowned, barely refraining from adding, *of course not.*

"You ride using intuition, experience. Heart, even." The woman tapped her fist against her chest. "And that's very much like what I'm doing."

"How so?"

"Everyone is so convinced that the only path forward is science, so they hand it all over to artificial intelligence."

"What's wrong with taking advantage of algorithms and sensors?"

"Nothing. But given the supply issues we've been having, how long will we keep getting raw materials for 3D printers? And is fabbing up sensors ultimately destined for failure the best use for them?"

Though Avery had asked herself the same questions, hearing them from someone else put her on the defensive. "What's the alternative?"

"Draw on the wisdom of the past. Use your eyes, and hands, and heart."

Avery raised her eyebrows. "But not to use any instrumentation—"

"Who said that? I have a handheld moisture meter that's lasted for years. But I let common sense, experience, and the know-how of those who came before me dictate what I plant and when. The proof is there." Madelaine pointed at the trophy. "But nobody wants to listen. They think they just need to figure out the right algorithm, and they'll produce vegetables that surpass mine. And maybe they could. But I wouldn't bet on it."

"Hey, Avery."

Avery turned to see her friend Gina approaching.

"Thought I might find you here," Gina said. "Ready to check out the midway?"

"Sure am." Avery turned to face Madelaine. "Look, I appreciate your time. Congratulations on your win." She nodded toward the trophy.

"Thanks," Madelaine said. "If you're ever interested in learning more about companion planting, look me up."

"I may just do that."

Avery turned away and followed Gina toward the exit, pondering the conversation with Madelaine.

Was the other woman right? Did her planting methods give her an advantage?

Maybe Sunset Valley Farms just has exceptionally good soil. That, Avery could believe.

Besides, why turn your back on progress? It didn't make sense.

"Hey, I hear they've added a few new rides," Gina said.

"Cool." Avery grinned. Now *that* was progress she could get behind.

∽ • ∾

Three days later, Avery stood at the start line for the women's two-hour bike relay, her muscles tense.

To the riders' left, brilliantly colored pennants with the logos of the fifteen towns that made up the Region snapped in the breeze. The teams would have wind to contend with as well as hills. Maybe that would work out to Windham's advantage. They'd trained in all kinds of weather, for this very reason.

Avery thought of what awaited her. The two-hour bike relay required a team of riders to take turns cycling along a course leading from the fairgrounds up through the town's hills and valleys. At the end of each loop, the cyclists would rocket around the track that had once been the site of harness horse races, until they arrived at the transfer section where the next rider on the team awaited the slap on the back that would signal them to begin their run. The team that completed the most laps would be declared the victor.

She'd volunteered to be the lead cyclist for the Windham team. It was a way to get out the prerace jitters, quickly.

Avery turned toward her teammates, waiting in the standby corral. Gina, the quintessential all-around athlete who could have participated, and starred, in any number of sports, but chose to hang out with their circle of friends. Jussie, waiting with set jaw, her brown hair peeking out from under her bike helmet. And Erryn, rock-solid and dependable.

She didn't want to let them down.

If she was honest with herself, that wasn't her only motivation today. She'd love to put in a performance that would impress the scouts, particularly the Toronto Tech rep she'd seen taking a seat in the stands a few minutes ago.

Avery shot another look up at the viewing area. Her muscles tensed. There, taking a seat beside the Toronto Tech scout, was Malvin Annson. What was he up to?

Forget it, she told herself. She turned her attention to the opposition. Familiar, for the most part, though she was certain she'd never raced against the woman next to her.

The other woman wore the uniform of the Lynnville team. Her dark hair showed under her bike helmet, and her face—

Avery frowned. She knew she'd never met the other woman before, but felt like she should know who she was. Why, though?

The web search I did to find out more about Malvin Annson. That's his daughter, Lona.

Noticing Avery's attention, Lona grinned. She called out, just loud enough for Avery to hear, "If you're looking to impress the Toronto Tech scout in the stands, he's here to see me. He's an old friend of my father's."

Avery gripped the handlebars so tightly that her hands hurt. *Just how much sway does Malvin Annson have?* In as neutral a tone as she could manage, she said, "I imagine he's here to see a lot of people."

"My father isn't one to cross," Lona said. "He generally gets what he wants."

And what he wants is to keep Mom and me over a barrel. So he can convince us to sell the farm. Maybe he wouldn't draw the line at trying to influence a scout's decision . . .

"Riders, take your marks."

Stewing in her own thoughts, Avery barely noticed the starter's words.

Her efforts could all be for nothing. *Maybe no matter how well I perform, I won't get a scholarship.*

The gun sounded to start the race, and Avery shot forward.

Riders sped along the straightaway and out into the blocked-off streets in a tight pack. Gradually, the pack thinned out into a line, with Lona in the lead. The Lynnville rider was, Avery noted, setting a killer pace.

If I fall behind now, I might never make up the distance.

We could lose the race. We could lose the farm. I could lose my chance to get out of here and go to university.

With these thoughts pounding at her, Avery brimmed with nervous energy. Consumed by the need to stay close to Lona, she sped along just behind the other woman, panting up the hill climbs and struggling to regain her breath on the flats. Halfway through the race, Avery's muscles tingled. By the time she reached the changeover area to tap Gina, sending her off on the second lap, Avery's sides ached.

When Avery entered the corral, Jussie looked at her quizzically. "That wasn't the game plan," she said in a mild tone.

"We didn't know Lona was going to go out so quickly."

"She likely trained for that. We didn't. And neither did they." Jussie nodded toward the Doverton rider who'd been in the first group along with Lona and Avery and had crossed the line just behind them. The Doverton woman was bent over double, trying to catch her breath.

She looks spent.

And I bet I don't look much better . . .

Now that she was back in the corral, with the spurt of anger that had lashed at her throughout the first lap ebbing, Avery's muscles felt leaden.

"I didn't want to leave you guys with an insurmountable distance to catch up," Avery protested.

"I know," Jussie said. She swung her bike around and headed for the changeover area to await Gina's return. As she watched her go, Avery's spirits plummeted.

Why *had* she taken Lona's bait?

And more importantly, would they be able to win the race despite her blunder?

As the laps piled up, racers dragged themselves back to the corral, looking more and more haggard. Cheers rang out from the stands each time a rider entered the stadium to circle the oval.

Next up for Windham, Avery mounted her bike and checked the countdown clock. This would likely be the last lap. The crowd noise notched up, and Avery looked up at the big screen to see who was entering the stadium.

Please, let that be Erryn, she thought.

But the screen showed a rider wearing the red and white jersey of the Lynnville team.

Beside her, Lona chuckled. "Too bad for you, I guess," she said. "Well, I'll be seeing you." The Lynnville rider positioned herself in the changeover lane, waited for the backslap from her teammate, and rocketed away.

Another anticipatory roar, followed by shouts of encouragement. Avery looked up again. It was Erryn, alright, but she'd clearly reached the end of her energy reserves. The bike wobbled, just for a moment. Somehow, Erryn managed to pick up her pace. Avery positioned herself at the start of the transfer area, eyes forward.

Another roar from the crowd, another rider. *Somebody's right on our heels*, Avery thought. She glanced back to judge Erryn's approach, then started coasting forward.

Erryn tapped Avery's back. "Go get 'em," she rasped.

Avery's final lap, like the others that had preceded it, proved to be a slog. She forced herself through the uphills. As she pedaled doggedly on, Avery regretted going out so quickly in the first lap.

Still, she kept pedaling, head down, as she entered the stadium. She could just see Lona making the turn at the north end.

Before Lona reached the changeover area, the horn sounded, signaling the end of the race.

Avery coasted toward her friends. "Sorry," she said.

"Next year is the one that really counts," Gina replied.

Bold words, but Avery couldn't help feeling a pang when she saw the Toronto Tech rep chatting with Lona after the race.

After the medal ceremony, Jussie gestured toward the midway. "I think we've earned some fun. You coming, Avery?"

For a moment, Avery was tempted. But she also felt the need to find a quiet place to process her thoughts. "Maybe I'll catch up later."

Avery headed for the agricultural barn and felt a twinge of annoyance when she saw a visitor chatting with Claire.

Then she recognized Claire's guest. Her fists clenched at her sides, and it took all of her self-control to keep from stomping over.

Breathing hard, she forced herself to remain in place until Malvin Annson departed. Then she hurried toward the booth, noting her mother's scowl.

"What did he want?" Avery asked.

"The same as before. He seemed quite pleased with himself, for some reason." Claire turned to look at her daughter. "I'm afraid I lost my temper. That won't improve our situation."

"You're not the only one." Avery outlined what had happened in the race, then hung her head.

"Well, I can't very well scold you for having the same flaw as myself," Claire said. "The thing is, I'm wondering whether we should accept Malvin's offer. We sold our available produce, and it'll pay down some of the debt, but it won't be enough to clear it. And we still need money to buy materials to fab up new sensors for next year. Who knows what next year's growing season will hold? If we can't settle up by the due date . . ."

Avery shook her head. "There must be a way to avoid that! I could drop out of school. Try to get a job in town."

"You'll do no such thing." Claire's voice was firm.

"*You* have a second job, in the off season."

"To pay the bills, yes. But you need to stay in school." Claire forced a smile. "It's important to me that you have the same opportunities your father and I did."

Avery's shoulders slumped. *To work so hard, and have it not be enough . . .*

She gazed out over the expanse of booths and displays, and her eyes narrowed. She wasn't the only one who'd worked hard. Take Madelaine, for example. Surely, it must be more physically difficult to farm the way she did.

But I'll bet she spends more time in the fresh air.

And she doesn't need to spend time, and money, on sensors . . .

Avery drew a sharp breath. There was an idea there, a ray of light that might show them a way out of this after all.

But success would hang on a slim thread.

Avery hesitated. Should she share her idea with her mother?

She had to be sure of something else, first.

"Can you take a break tonight?"

Claire nodded, slowly. "I planned on it. Traffic should slow in an hour, during dinner time."

"Why don't we meet at the food court in the Homecraft Building? I might have an idea."

"I could use something to eat, I suppose," Claire admitted. "But—"

"See you there," Avery said.

She sped away before Claire could argue.

☙ • ❧

At the appointed time, Avery waited impatiently at her chosen table, trying to anticipate her mother's reaction. Now that she'd taken the initial steps to explore the feasibility of her idea, she wondered if she was being rash. Noticing that her palms were slick with sweat, Avery rubbed them on her upper thigh.

"Sorry I'm a bit late." Claire ran a hand through her hair. "I—"

Then she stopped and stared at the woman sitting opposite Avery.

"Hello, Claire," said Madelaine Stone.

"Hello, Madelaine," Claire said, her tone stiff. "It's been awhile."

Claire pulled out a chair and sat down. Then she turned to Avery, eyebrows raised.

"I asked Madelaine to join us," Avery said. "I think she can help."

Claire crossed her arms and turned to Madelaine. "We've butted heads in the past. Why would you help us out now?"

"I agree, you and I have often had different ways of doing things." Madelaine said the words without rancor. "But I don't like what Malvin Annson is up to any more than you do. It sets a bad precedent. If he's successful in pressuring one farmer, that'll make it that much more difficult for the rest of us. So I'm willing to let bygones be bygones."

Claire thought about it for a moment. Then she leaned forward. "Me too."

"Good," Madelaine said. "Now, I suggest we let Avery do the talking. It was, after all, her idea."

And Avery began her explanation, relieved to see her mother's intent expression as she listened.

∽ • ∾

Almost a year later, Avery wandered through the front fields, checking the readiness of the butternut squash. She closed her fist around a defective sensor she'd just replaced. She should be able to repair this one, but they'd better hope they didn't experience many more failures. It had been difficult to keep the front fields running properly.

Fortunately, they'd had a reserve of sensors to draw on through the summer. The front fields, the ones visible from the road, were the only ones managed by the AI this year.

A luxury sedan rumbled up the driveway leading to the storage barn. Avery's muscles tensed. *Right on cue.* It was almost a year ago that Malvin Annson had first approached her mother about selling the farm. Avery had seen Malvin's vehicle driving past several times during the summer as he checked out the fields.

Anticipating Malvin's interest, Avery had managed the crops accordingly. She'd allowed failed sensors to go unreplaced in certain sectors visible from the road so that patches of vegetation showed signs of stress. It was important that Malvin think he had them right where he wanted them until they could pay off the debt and remove him from the equation. Otherwise, he might feel compelled to come up with other strategies to make their lives difficult.

Avery watched as Claire Mackey emerged from the storage shed to converse with her visitor. Malvin's posture conveyed smugness, while Claire stood with downcast gaze and rounded shoulders.

Good, Avery thought. *Let him think we're down and out.*

Avery waited until Malvin had driven out of sight before swinging up on her bike to ride to the back acreage, which was shielded from the road by a windbreak.

She stopped the bike and surveyed the fields of mingled vegetables and flowers, listening to the hum of pollinators. They'd never had yields like this—nor had the fields ever looked so beautiful. But none of it would have been possible without Madelaine's help. She'd assisted Avery in deciding which crops to plant where. Avery shook her head, remembering how Madelaine had wandered through the field, explaining the reasons for her recommendations.

One day a week during the summer, Avery had worked side by side with Madelaine at Sunset Valley Farm, eager to absorb know-how. Some days, she'd felt like her head might explode.

Avery grinned ruefully as she turned toward the farmhouse. Hopefully, all that work would pay off.

$\backsim$ • $\backsim$

The day of the two-hour bike relay, Avery's heart jumped like a grasshopper as she headed toward the starting line.

Lona Annson greeted her with a knowing smirk. "They're trusting you to be the starting rider again? I thought they'd have learned better last year."

Avery let the remark ride. The matter of who should ride the lead lap had been a point of discussion with her teammates. But they'd agreed on a strategy and adjusted their training plan accordingly.

Lona continued to chatter, trying to goad Avery into impetuous behavior.

Avery sniped back just often enough to support the illusion that Lona had succeeded in getting under her skin.

Then the starter's gun popped, sending the riders off.

For a few hundred meters, Avery kept pace with Lona, pretending not to notice the other woman's gloating expression. But when they reached the first hill, she let Lona go ahead, grinning when she noticed that the other woman rode hard, as if Avery were still right behind her.

From there on, Avery followed the plan the team had laid out, staying within reach of Lona by conserving her energy on the hill climbs, then making up distance on the flats. She played cat and mouse, speeding up just often enough to send the other woman darting ahead, often at the start of uphill sections.

When Avery began what the clock suggested would be the last lap, only a few bike lengths separated the Windham team from the front-runners from Lynnville. By the time they returned to the fairgrounds, Avery had made up the distance. She and Lona rode side by side down the straightaway. Avery checked the countdown clock, then drew on reserves built up through the long summer laboring in the fields. She blew past Lona just before the horn sounded to end the race.

It took Avery time to get her breath back after completing the race. Her teammates' hearty backslaps set those efforts back, but she didn't mind. Gradually, her heart rate returned to normal.

Avery saw a short, wiry man who'd been leaning against the fence surrounding the corral walking toward her. The man wore a cap bearing the insignia of Guelph University.

A year ago, a scholarship offer such as the one the Guelph rep made would have seemed like a consolation prize. Now, she accepted it with a smile. Inspired by her experience in the fields this summer, she'd changed her first choice in the University Portal, dropping Toronto Tech in favor of schools offering courses in traditional agriculture.

After the Guelph University scout walked away, Avery glanced around the riders' corral. *Last time I'll be here*, she thought, feeling a pang.

She'd achieved her dream, and yet, it didn't feel the way she'd expected.

Avery's expression grew somber when she remembered that a scholarship wasn't the only thing at stake. With her heart beating faster, Avery made her way to the Agricultural Building.

∽ • ∾

"We did it."

Although those three words were what she'd hoped to hear, Avery stared at her mother in disbelief.

"I've made the deposits already. The loan's been cleared."

Avery grinned. "And I got a scholarship, too. To Guelph."

Claire forced a smile. It might have fooled someone who didn't know her, but Avery wasn't taken in.

"What's wrong with Guelph?" Avery crossed her arms as she awaited her mother's response.

"Nothing. It's just—it wasn't what you wanted, at first. Are you sure you're not settling?"

Avery shook her head. "The truth is, I enjoy working in the fields more than I expected. I think we should use Madelaine's methods going forward."

"It's hard to argue with success."

Despite her bold words, Avery felt a twinge of uncertainty. *Was* she sure about leaving the AI-governed farming methods behind in favor of the traditional ways?

She thought about the workshop where she'd toiled on the sensors and felt a pang of guilt. Maybe she was being unfaithful to the memory of her father. Was she right to give up on the opportunity to spend time in the place where they'd shared so many happy hours?

He's gone now. And you can't keep doing the same things, over and over, for the sake of nostalgia.

Claire gave her daughter a shrewd look, as though she could deduce her thoughts. "I'm proud of you," she said. "And your father would be, too."

Avery squared her shoulders. There were worse things than riding the fields in the sunshine, testing the dirt with your own hands, and standing back and surveying a field of companion crops abuzz with pollinators.

Far worse things.

She smiled.

A BOAT, A BIKE, AND A BALLOON
∽ MARTA PELRINE-BACON ∾

Amelia Fare lived in a house on a cliff between the barren lands and the sea. Her parents locked her in a tower room to keep her safe. They'd worked hard to find the safest room in all the land. Hadn't they told her often enough how thieves and other evils were always hunting?

For her sixteenth birthday, they asked Amelia what she wanted most. Freedom was out of the question, so she asked for a garden.

Her parents whispered in the hallway. No. A garden meant going outside. A flower, they said. She could have a flower, yellow like a sun, to put in her window. Why have a garden with things that sting or slither when she could have a single perfect blossom? And didn't she see how sickly the sun was in the cloudy sky? What could possibly grow?

Besides, a girl didn't need dirt under her fingernails or sweat on the back of her neck.

They promised that the flower would never wilt. It would close when she was sleeping and open when she awoke. Amelia thanked her parents, and she kissed the perfect yellow bloom before setting it on the windowsill. That was when the trouble began.

Amelia wondered where her parents had gotten the yellow flower. She'd never seen a town or a shop. She'd read about them in books, but as she felt the soft green of the flower's leaves, she couldn't completely imagine what a flower shop might look like. What did a city look like? What did anything look like beyond the horizon that encircled her days?

The sea went on in one direction and the barren lands in the other. The flower wasn't a simple gift. It watched her every move across the room and stared at her pictures and books. "Are you a spy or a companion?" she asked.

The breeze through the window caused the flower to nod.

$$\infty \cdot \infty$$

The breeze continued as it always did from over the sea. What was on the other side of the sea?

"Nothing," her mother said.

"Terrors," said her father.

"But what does that mean?" Amelia asked. "You never say."

"The truth will give you bad dreams," her mother said. "And it's our job to protect you from bad dreams."

"Sorry. Look, darling daughter, speak of this again and I'll throw you from the window."

Her mother nodded. "If that's the only way to protect you."

"But—" Amelia began, unsure if she believed this threat and wishing someone would protect her from them.

Her father reached for her hair. He turned his hand so that a thick lock of hair wrapped around his wrist. Her hair was long, almost to the floor. He studied its brightness and let it spill from his fingers. "The world is a better place when it is ignorant of treasure," he finally said. "We gave you the flower you asked for. Now's not the time to show you to the world."

Amelia told her dreams to the flower. She told the flower how she wanted to see the world, and how one day she might throw herself from her window just to end her boredom. "It isn't as if I'm really living, after all, is it?" she asked the yellow bloom.

The flower did as her parents said it would. It slept when she slept and woke when she woke, and when she talked, it listened. Its petals brightened when it listened until she could barely stand to look at it directly.

"Where are you from?" Amelia asked. "I'd love to see where you're from and all the flowers you grew up with. How beautiful the place must be."

The flower nodded more in the breeze.

"Do you miss it?" She gazed out her window. She could see the barren side of her world if she walked out into the hall—she was sometimes allowed—and looked out the window there, but the emptiness made her lonelier still. The sand blew around their home in swirls and flurries. When her parents headed out in that direction, they wrapped themselves in many cloths and said three prayers to protect themselves on the way.

The sea glistened and undulated. Dolphins sometimes broke the surface as did flying fish. They weren't much, but they were all she had for 16 years. When her parents headed in that direction, bundled in their tiny boat, they said different prayers for protection.

"If I could get out of this tower," she said, "I'd take you with me. I'd take you back to your garden, and it would be my first quest." She leaned back on her bed. "Every girl needs a quest, don't you think?"

Amelia dozed off. She was supposed to be studying trigonometry and the history of the moon, but she felt no hurry to learn these things. She had the rest of her life to study.

When she awoke, the dismal sun was low, its light not quite sparkling on the sea. She stretched and yawned. She looked to her flower to see its warm glow and gasped. The clay pot the flower was rooted in was cracked. Cracks ran in several directions.

"What has happened to you?" she cried. Then she saw the root dangling from the pot's side. The root went out the window and down the tower to the rocks below. "Oh, my love," she said. She'd been calling it that for some time now. "Are you all right?"

The flower nodded in the breeze.

"How did you do that?" Amelia leaned over the flower to take a better look at the ground. "How could you have had so much root in such a small pot? Didn't it hurt?"

The root swayed in the breeze.

"You must feel better, but . . ." She studied the cracks and almost touched them. "Isn't that dangerous? Your soil will spill out and then you'll die."

In her desk she found tape, and, carefully so as not to break the clay any further, she pulled the tape around the pot and secured the pieces into place. The breeze picked up, and the flower and its leaves moved vigorously. "What?" she asked. "What are you trying to tell me?"

She looked down the side of the tower again. The root seemed strong. She'd never seen a rope in real life, but the root put the word in her mind.

The last of the sun's poor light shone on the water before it set behind the horizon. Each wave of the water beckoned like a whispered promise. "Yes, of course," Amelia said. "I'll take you to your garden. That's exactly what I'll do."

Amelia climbed onto the windowsill, took the root in one hand, and climbed out the window, the breeze lifting her skirt and her hair and the waves calling from below.

Her parents' small boat knocked against the rocks. Her stomach lurched as she jerked downward, but the root held and the pot didn't tip. Fear and excitement gave her strength. Night grew around her, and she moved silently down to the earth. For years her parents had talked about magic, but this was the first time she felt magic was real.

Feet on the ground, Amelia tugged on the root one more time. The flowerpot tilted and fell. She caught the flower in her arms. The yellow glowed, and she inspected the pot and the bloom. No further damage had been done.

Her first time out of the tower made her dizzy. There was, however, no time to breathe deeply and think. She made her way to the boat.

Amelia knew nothing about sailing. She struggled with the rigging, and the boat pitched sideways. She tumbled around, but she held the rope and the wind turned. A few moments later, the boat cut smoothly through the water, and Amelia watched the clouds. She imagined they called to her. She imagined feeling their apparent softness against her face.

The nighttime sea dragged the boat away from the tower and the world Amelia knew. The length of root rested in the boat, but it seemed to have gotten much shorter. She didn't really notice. The world was too interesting.

The water was cool to her fingers, and her fingers, after being in the water, tasted of salt. It was true! The sea was salty indeed. The boat rose and dipped, and this, she realized, was motion. Her stomach turned slightly. She gripped the sides of the boat until her fingers stiffened. "Look at it all," Amelia said to her flower. "Is this the way you came? Do you remember the sea?"

Finally, she let go of the sides of the boat to lift the flower up over her head. "Do you see the world, my love?" she asked. "It's beautiful."

With the motion of the boat, the flower nodded.

Amelia had no sense of time, but eventually the boat drifted in sight of the shore. City lights twinkled and sparkled. "Wow," she whispered. "People can make the night look like that?" Music like nothing she'd ever heard met her as the boat slid up on the beach.

She held the flower closer to her thumping heart. All these years believing she wanted to hear other people, and now she heard new voices. She was so far from the safety of her room.

"I shall be brave," she told her flower.

Amelia climbed out of the boat, getting her feet wet, but she hardly noticed. For the first time, she worried about her dress and her hair. What if she looked different? What if someone spoke to her? What if they asked her about her parents?

There was laughter. The people laughing had lives, and they knew many rooms and places and each other. All she had was her tower and her parents who didn't laugh like that. Or maybe they did. What did she know of their lives beyond the tower? Maybe they had friends. Maybe they laughed like that too when they were far away from her.

The flower felt warm in her hands. "I'll stick to the shadows," she said. "I've read that in books. Besides, a garden won't be filled with laughing people, right? I bet your garden is quiet and solitary." She headed down the beach, and with each step, the flower seemed warmer and warmer.

They reached a path that led up a hill, and at the top of that hill stood a wall and a gate. "Is it as easy as this?" she asked her flower. "Could your garden be on the other side?"

It was not that easy.

On the other side of the gate, Amelia found a path through a junkyard. Shadows loomed around twisted contraptions of metal and moonlight struck edges of metal and glass. "What is this place?" She stood and looked off over the field of abandoned and left-behind things. She couldn't see that far ahead.

Her stomach growled. Of course, she had no food. Well, I have to keep going. There is no going back.

The yellow flower nodded towards the path, and when the path forked, it nodded in the direction she should take. Once, a piece of metal bent onto the path and scratched her leg. She winced but didn't bother to check for blood. Going forward was all that mattered in a quest.

The root, much shorter now, was still long enough to drag on the ground behind her. But Amelia paid no attention to the line it left in the dirt.

The world was quiet now. Amelia and her flower walked down an alley. Suddenly came a sound she'd not heard before:

the crush of wheels crunching to a halt on pebbles and dirt. "That's a bike!" She'd seen pictures.

A boy sat atop the contraption. "Oi. I coulda run you right down. Watch where you're going or don't go."

"Is it hard to ride?" she asked, oblivious to the boy's annoyance. The flower's root had wrapped around her waist.

"What's it to you?"

Amelia blinked. She was talking to a boy! She was talking to someone who wasn't her parents! "Hello," she said. She looked from the bike to the boy and back to the bike. The bike was far more interesting. The flower's root tugged around her waist, and she realized the bike was more useful. "May I ride it? I have a long ways to go."

"What? Are you mad? I'd give you my liver before I'd let you ride my bike."

Amelia made a face. "I don't need a liver."

The boy snorted. "Besides. Girls don't ride bikes. Everyone knows that."

Now, Amelia hadn't been raised to get along with other children. She knew how to say thank you and please and she read about well-behaved children in books, but the city air and sounds, the boy's glare and morning shadows between the narrow streets, and smells of too many things she didn't recognize overwhelmed her. So she followed through on her very first impulse.

Amelia Fare charged at him, taking him quite by surprise and knocking him clear off his bike. He sprawled on the grimy street, the wind knocked out of him.

Amelia dropped the flowerpot in the bike's basket and swung her leg over the seat. Of course, she didn't know what she was doing and skidded sideways immediately. She righted herself, then twisted and nearly pitched over the handlebars. The boy was pushing himself up and shaking his head. He winced when he moved.

The flower, its root now firmly around her waist, pulled at her, and she found her balance. Seconds later, she was flying down the street, her skirts flapping, her hair streaming, and the boy's shouts disappearing behind her.

The flower, in its cracked pot, bounced along in the woven basket, but another of its roots looped into the weave. It seemed secure enough, more secure than Amelia, in fact. She bounced along, unsteady and frequently swerving.

Where the streets divided or turned, she'd slow down enough for the flower to nod in one direction or another, then she hurried on. Sometimes, someone would point and shout. The boy was apparently not the only one who thought bikes weren't for girls. These must've been her parents' people, she reasoned, since they thought so little was for girls as well.

Her legs and her lungs ached, but she kept on. The flower's yellow brightened. Finally, the morning murky light pooling over the houses, Amelia and the flower reached a high wall. In the wall was a wrought iron gate, thickly covered in dark green vines. Sweaty and aching, Amelia brought the bike to a jolting halt. The metal frame was hot under her hands. She stumbled off it, scooping up the flower before letting the bike fall to the ground.

The gate was locked.

Hunger pains and thirst wedged through Amelia's insides. "Oh, I hope there's something to eat over there," she mumbled as she moved closer to the gate. She tried to peer through the vines but saw only shades of green. She had one hand at the stitch in her side and the other around the flowerpot. A root reached from the soil to a nearly hidden lock. There came a click, and the gate eased open just enough.

Amelia pushed her way through. She was sweating profusely now. She wasn't used to it. Her tower room had always been cool, and her parents never allowed her to exert herself. "It isn't safe," they said. "You'll burn up."

But it felt good to wipe sweat from her brow and feel the coolness of the breeze.

On the other side of the gate, she found a vast, gently sloping plain. In the distance were mountains, and the flower nodded to the highest peak. Amelia considered going back for the bike, but it wouldn't get her up the cliffs. It was a shame. She'd rather enjoyed that wild ride through the streets, nearly crashing into people and walls.

But as she braced herself for the long trek to the mountains, she spotted a man waving. Next to him sat a large basket, and behind, a wide stretch of colored cloth. Amelia, curious, approached. As much as she wanted to find the flower's garden and a meal, the world was endlessly interesting. She wished to see all of it after seeing the flower home.

"Like a ride up into the clouds?" the man asked.

"I don't understand. You're not a bird."

The man guffawed. "I like a girl with a sense of humor! Haven't you ever seen a balloon before?"

Of course, she hadn't. She eyed the basket and the strange metal bits. She could think only of party balloons she'd read about in books, but nothing like this. "That'll take you up to the sky?"

"Absolutely. Great views. Perfectly safe. Reasonable prices."

Amelia looked up. The sun barely lit up the vast grassland around them. "Can we reach the sun?"

"You just can't stop with the jokes, can you, lass? No. Can't go up that high. If we could, we would fix the sun, wouldn't we?"

"What do you mean? What's wrong with it?"

The man's jovial expression faltered, but he fixed it right again. "Guess you're too young to remember when the sun was bright and hot. That's a sickly sun we got up there. Why, it used to be so warm, so yellow, like that flower you got there. But no more. No more." He rubbed his hands together. "We got to make the best of it though, don't we? It's a lot easier for me to fly my balloon these days. All I need is passengers. So, what do you say, little lady?"

"But how do you get passengers out here? The city's on the other side of that gate. And it was locked."

He couldn't hide his surprise. "You come from that city on the other side of the gate? No one's come through there for years." He studied her. The soft sunlight cast soft shadows on his face. His gold buttons didn't gleam like they should. "But what have you, girl, there's other towns and city folk. They come out here. Only place for my balloon to fit. Can't exactly fit her on city streets, can I? Now. How about a ticket?"

Amelia's thoughts sped. She saw the balloon could help her reach the top of the mountain, but she had no money. "How does it work?" she asked.

"You've got to buy a ticket, miss."

"Oh. Well. I can't buy a ticket until I know it works." Amelia was grateful for the many books she'd read. The various stories gave her helpful ideas.

The man hesitated, but he couldn't resist showing off his pride and joy. Soon he had the burner going and the lines set. Seeing Amelia's eyes light up as the balloon took on its full shape pleased him.

The balloon reached its full height, and Amelia craned her neck to take it in. It was glorious in its rainbow of color. Then the man turned his back to check one of the stakes in the ground.

The flower, ever warmer in her hands, nodded, and Amelia leapt forward. She clambered into the basket, and before the man could turn back and say anything more about a ticket, the roots of the flower lashed out in four directions, undoing the stakes and setting the balloon free.

Never before had anyone, and certainly not a girl, gotten so far in stealing his balloon, and it took precious seconds for him to recover from the shock. The seconds cost him, and when he lunged to grab a rope, it was too late. The wind had them, and up they went, away from the cursing man, toward the calling mountain.

Amelia soon realized she had no control over the balloon. It wasn't like the boat or the bike. There was no way to steer. But the wind seemed kindly towards her and set to carrying her to the very peak the flower pointed to. So, Amelia took to enjoying the ride.

The height made her giddy. She wished to climb higher and higher. The city, even in the dusty light of the sickly sun, looked like a jewel in the earth, and beyond that she glimpsed the gray water of the sea. Perhaps if they'd gone higher, she'd have seen the tower her parents had kept her in. They must be looking for her. She smiled. They'd never think to look up!

As much as she'd wanted to reach the mountain, she was disappointed to have her flight come to an end. A bit of frost coated the edges of the basket, but the flower kept her warm. And once the balloon touched down on the mountaintop, all hints of chill vanished. In fact, she climbed out of the basket, surprised at the heat.

The wind returned and lifted up the balloon. Amelia sighed with relief. She hoped the man would have his contraption back. She hadn't wanted to be a thief.

Then she turned around to see her destination.

A universe of yellow flowers greeted her. And every bloom turned to see her standing with the cracked flowerpot in her arms. Yellow light flooded over them. Yellow roses, lilies, tulips, daffodils, carnations, and orchids. Amelia recognized some of them from books, but the rest were strangers to her. Her yellow flower danced from its roots. "This is home, isn't it, love?"

The flowers were beautiful. She didn't think she'd ever look away.

A gust of wind struck them, and it sounded as if it were blowing over hollow tubes. Clouds moved overhead, but Amelia didn't notice. The flowers were too bright.

"Who is so brave to enter my garden without an invitation? Who even could?"

Amelia jumped. A woman stood on the path. Her dress was yellow and her skin the color of a vine's branches. "What brings . . ." The woman stopped. "You've one of my flowers."

"Yes. My parents gave it to me." Amelia considered holding the flower out to her. Returning the flower to the garden had been the reason for the journey, but faced with the possibility of losing the brightness beside her, she hesitated. "I wanted to see where it came from."

"Your parents?" The woman strode over and leaned in toward Amelia. "Where are you from, child?"

The knowingness in the woman's eyes frightened Amelia. "Across the sea." The woman's gaze burned through her, and Amelia felt more seen than ever in her life.

"And you bring me back my stolen child?" the woman asked.

Amelia's heart fluttered. "I . . . I don't know if it was stolen or not. But it asked me to bring it home."

"Come closer," the woman said.

"Are you a witch?"

"Are you?"

The question startled Amelia. "I'm Amelia Fare."

"And you speak to flowers and find your way here from across the sea."

Now Amelia stepped closer to the woman. "Only because I didn't want to be locked in my room."

The woman, all luminous shades of brown and gold, specks of green flashing in her eyes, knelt down. "And what do you think of the world you've seen so far, there beyond the mountain?"

Amelia thought about what she'd seen, the narrow streets and the boat, the bike, and the balloon. "It's not what I expected."

"It never is."

Amelia held out the cracked flowerpot. The shining flower nodded its head toward the woman. "Here," Amelia said. "Your child."

The woman laughed, her eyes glinting. "I didn't mean the flower." And with that, she reached for Amelia. As Amelia was pulled into her arms, warmth like she'd never known enveloped her, and the flowerpot dropped from her hands. The roots broke free of the remains of the pot and thrust themselves into the ground. All the blooms in the garden nodded in the growing breeze.

Light, burning and gold, poured from their embrace. Amelia felt herself lifted from the ground, and for the first time in sixteen years, true sunlight bathed the world. The man, the boy, all the citizens of all the cities and towns, and even the two who had pretended to be her parents looked up into blinding brightness.

"I meant you," said the woman, lifting Amelia up to the sky and letting her go. "My daughter, the sun."

THE WIND THAT WHISPERED THROUGH THE TREES

∾ J.D. HARLOCK ∾

With the grace of the gentle winds that blew past her and eyes as wide as the picturesque pastures before her, Aleyna rode up and down the slopes of Marj al Shams on her very own bicycle. This was no ordinary bicycle powered by the sun, but one of those curious relics from another time that needed her to pedal. Still, it worked like a charm, feeling as natural to her as treading water was to the garganeys that swam past her or burrowing was to the honey badgers she passed by.

What she didn't pass by, however, were the residents of Southern Lebanon, who seemed nowhere to be found. So it was a welcome sight when she spotted a saj stand in the middle of a crossroad one quiet afternoon. Aleyna parked the bicycle in the rack to the side of the shack, rang the bell hanging from the roof, and waited in one of the chairs for someone to arrive.

Soon after, the saj baker hobbled down the curved terrain to the stand. Removing his tattered coat and fingerless gloves, he pointed toward the menu above him without saying a word, and Aleyna responded with her order. Carefully, he poured the batter onto the stove's mound, then added cheese and thyme as he sang an old Arabic tune that hit a little too close to home:

And I'll leave it all behind

To wherever I have in mind;

For that is what you do

When the wind whispers to you . . .

As she dug into her roll, savoring the akkawi cheese and wild thyme, she took a moment to admire the natural wonders all around her.

"Are you from here?" the saj baker asked, studying her face. "Ah, I'd recognize those eyes anywhere. You're—"

Aleyna nodded.

The man then went through the motions, asking her what became of her family, where they were now, and how things were going, but when he got those answers, he frowned: "Why return?"

And all Aleyna had to say was: "Because the wind whispered to me."

᠔ • ᠔

Veering off the well-worn path, she rode toward the river, wondering if it was all as she recalled it. When she reached the bend, she carefully rested the bicycle against the safety fence, lest it fall into the glade, and sat under the shade of an olive tree. After inspecting the bark for the name she'd once carved there, she pulled out her handcrafted journal from her backpack and stared at a new blank page for only a moment before finally pouring her heart into each word again as she once had when she was a child sitting beneath this very tree. Whether it was the fragrance of the blooming jasmines or the vista of the melting snowcaps, she could not tell you. All she knew was that it was here, and only here, that the hushed tones of yearned inspiration rustled through the leaves all around her and allowed her to write to her heart's content. Even after yet another prolonged war, Southern Lebanon hadn't changed, and she was thankful for that. That is until her phone rang . . .

"Did interviewing Ms. Jbara go well?" Grandma Rashida seemed just as worried as she was when Aleyna informed her she was heading back to Lebanon. "You didn't upset her, did you? Salim was explicit about this when I asked her for this favor."

"Teta," Aleyna groaned, checking her watch. Really, some things about Southern Lebanon never changed. "You called this morning, and I told you it'll take place later today. What exactly are you so worried about?"

"Oh, just leave the poor old woman alone," Grandma Rashida clicked her tongue, exasperated. "I know you're a fan of her writing, but Salma Jbara does not have to explain to anyone why she chose to share her story with the world. Even if we still can't figure it out, we should at least have the decency not to pry into the matter anymore."

"It's important that we know," Aleyna clapped back with uncharacteristic confidence. "This is our history, and she's inspired so many of us to write over the years. I can't imagine where I would be if I hadn't read *Nowhere Road* after we left."

Grandma Rashida sighed. "Couldn't the magazine have had you report on something else?"

"I chose this," Aleyna responded, enunciating every word. "I pitched the interview, and I'm not just delivering the same old article about her."

"But why? And why now? Rumors have been swirling about it in the village for decades. Each one is more troubling than the last. If she wanted to explain herself, she would've, and I'm afraid this isn't the life-changing experience you're expecting."

Aleyna winced. "It's the anniversary of her first and only publication . . . and I'm sorry, Teta, but we need to know."

∽ • ∾

The poetess lived in a cabin at the far edge of the village on land flattened generations ago. There were no trees, only crisply cut grass, and one wind turbine that powered her home with more electricity than she would ever need. As instructed by her supervisors, Aleyna parked her bike out of sight of the abode and put away her electronics in the front basket. Unable to find a doorbell, she knocked gently, expecting the woman herself, only to be met by a thin man with a pencil mustache and slicked-back hair. Aleyna introduced herself, but the man did not immediately step aside to allow her in: "My name is Salim, and I'm an old friend of your family's, which is why I allowed this interview with my mother, but I must warn you to be careful. I know this date was probably chosen intentionally, but the anniversary is difficult for her. Please keep that in mind," he whispered into her ear before ushering her in.

Aleyna followed him, passing shelves and shelves of unpublished handwritten manuscripts that would cause a stir in the literary community if she were to report on them. Expecting her to have her nose in a typewriter in her study, Aleyna was startled to find the poetess in a daze, staring blankly into space.

"Madam Salma Jbara," Aleyna placed her hand on her chest as a respectful greeting. "My name is Aleyna Gholmieh, and I'm a fan writing a feature on you for *The Old Orient* for the anniversary of your first publication. I read it after we left for America, and it changed my life in more ways than you can imagine."

Hearing this, Salma went quiet for a moment, but before Aleyna could say more, she broke out into a dry laugh.

"I can't believe it's been long enough that we can celebrate an anniversary," Salma muttered. Before Aleyna could take her seat. Salma instructed her to head to the cabinet near the door and pick whichever bottle piqued her interest. Choosing one of the few with more than half its contents, she handed it over to Salma, who had wine glasses ready on the desk.

"It's been a long time since I've been interviewed, but let me guess . . ." Salma sucked at her cheeks. "You'll ask the questions everyone's always wanted the answers to, the ones I've never answered—who I am, why I write, and how on earth I had it in me to publish *Nowhere Road* back then with all of that going on."

Aleyna wasn't sure how to respond, but she knew to play it safe. Putting the cup of wine down, she straightened her back and recited the rehearsed lines.

"These subjects may be touched on, but our readers are expats interested in learning about anything related to Lebanon's cultural history. Most of them are around my age, so they aren't familiar with events that took place that far back and would love to have an authentic firsthand account of our collective past, even if you've answered these questions before."

"Then, let's carry on . . ." Salma tapped her thighs playfully as Salim left the room. Aleyna pulled out a recorder to capture this moment she had waited for her entire life, holding the journal to preserve her thoughts in the moment. Starting with a round of formulaic questions, Aleyna asked Salma the standard fluff while making notes of whatever came into her head, hoping she could ease Salma into some of the later, more introspective ones before finally posing the question on everyone's mind. However, after receiving a series of rambling responses in a drunk haze, Aleyna impatiently blurted it out. "Would you be willing to tell us why you chose to come forward and publish *Nowhere Road* all those years ago? It was so brave of you, and I think we need to know. I've been wondering for so long. . . ."

Of course, Aleyna expected pushback, but Salma smiled calmly and nodded.

"Oh, I'm not sure if I should, dear. I mean, that's always been an odd question for me." Aleyna pressed on. "I didn't see a reason to answer it because if others were as curious as they said they were, it wouldn't have been difficult to find out what had happened. You see, a bombing took place not far from here only a couple of days before I announced my retirement. Look here. . . ." She pushed back the chair and pulled up her gown. Much to Aleyna's shock, her left leg was gone.

"Couldn't you wear a prosthetic—"

"I can, but I won't. I'm not sure why, to be honest. Forests cleared out for failed endeavors are never replanted, are they? Sometimes you need to remember, and sometimes you can't help but remember." The old woman walked over to the sliding doors that led to the garden and pulled up the blinds. "I couldn't believe it, but I wasn't the one targeted. It was just fate. I was just cycling back home when the blast occurred, and then . . . and then . . . I lost him."

Aleyna said nothing as Salma broke down in front of her.

 ∽ • ∾

Escorted to the patio so Salma could recollect herself, Aleyna stood on the pavement in the bitter twilight, staring silently at the hills of Southern Lebanon that seemed so inviting just earlier that day. It never occurred to her that this was how she would finally find the answer to her lifelong question, and she wondered why she had ever asked the question in the first place. At a loss, she reached for the journal in her satchel to try to make sense of her feelings, only to realize that she had left it back in the study.

Salma considered sneaking back inside for it, but Salim returned with a vase and an assortment of sweets.

"Give her some time to calm down. I'm sorry you had to witness that. I tried explaining this to your grandmother, but it was hard to put into words," Salim said, handing her a cup of rosewater and clinking it against his. "This should soothe your nerves."

More than anything, Aleyna found it odd that Salim stood there collected, minding his thoughts, and staring at a monument composed of rusted bicycle parts erected in the center of the garden.

"Aleyna, was it?" Salim motioned towards the platform. "Inspect the inscription, and that should clear everything up."

Hesitantly, Aleyna trod toward the monument and kneeled to read what was written as the howling currents rumbled above her. It was a passage familiar to anyone who had read *Nowhere Road*, and it resonated with her now more than it ever had before:

"Cycling down an overgrown path, you lose sight of the destination."

A memorial then followed it:

"In memory of an unborn child."

Once Salma had taken her medication, Aleyna was allowed back inside to continue the interview, but she had already resolved to hand in a puff piece that only met the uninspiring demands of the magazine editorial. This article could never resonate with the younger readers of *The Old Orient* who were inspired by *Nowhere Road* as she had hoped it would, but she was at peace with that. Before Aleyna could tell her that there was no longer a need to continue the interview, she noticed that Salma had spectacles and was reading from her journal. Knowing better than to chastise a woman her age for this intrusion after what just happened, Aleyna sat down quietly and watched her read. There was a curious expression on Salma's face that Aleyna couldn't quite put her finger on, but the old woman seemed serene for the first time since she'd met her.

"Now what," she thought as she rolled her bicycle up the hill alongside the zephyr. Facing the road ahead, Aleyna wondered what path would unfold for her. From where she stood, the road seemed to stretch on forever, frightening and exciting her in equal measure. With this bike, she could now choose a new destination and ride on until she finally found someplace to settle.

Then, maybe, she could write her own stories. . . .

But what would she write about?

Maybe, she would write about this.

Yes, maybe she would write about all of this: the return to Lebanon, the conversation with the old woman, and the wind that whispered to her through the trees.

DEEP ROOTS SANCTUARY

✍ JOE BIEL ✍

I was on my way back from the nursery with many saplings precariously balanced under one branch. I rolled up to the stop sign and tried to track stand, but a flicker of noise caught my attention in the distance. I planted my foot firmly on the earth. The incessant wail of human traffic captured my attention, and I waited too long.

My roots started to take hold, cracking through the pavement and mounting themselves below. The elder treents had warned me about this, but it was too late. Something had changed for my people over the past year due to the changing climate: If we didn't keep moving, the ground would reclaim our roots. And we'd be stuck.

I was now firmly rooted, and there were cracks ten feet in every direction across the broken pavement. I wiggled my upper torso and rotated my trunk. For some reason, our hybrid root system only goes halfway up our spine.

This was the only major road connecting my village to the next city, so I knew that any oncoming traffic would have to go right over my cracked concrete.

I was petrified, figuring this was likely the end of me. I would be run over here, out in the middle of nowhere, on a road I had traversed what felt like millions of times. I just stood there with a trunk full of saplings, waiting to be steamrolled by a distracted driver. What else could I do?

Over the following week, I accepted my fate and decided that I could attempt to twist it, even if I couldn't budge below my torso. I began surveying my surroundings. My bicycle's welded joints had snapped under the sheer size of my powerful trunk, and I was gaining height despite my sheer lack of terminal velocity. I guess I assumed that once I stopped moving, I would get wider. Instead, I only got taller. I was still learning about biology and science well into my 100th year, I guess.

Before long, I could see deep into the distance. It was the same noise that I had heard a week earlier. The horns coalesced into a single obnoxious wail. I heard the friction of their heavy loads and the rancid stench of their noxious fumes continuing to destroy my native environs. It was even worse than I thought. A brigade of rogue truckers were amassing. A month prior, a similar convoy had merely driven in circles around me, as if this asserted dominance or anything at all. Now, they were heading my way. Ugh.

The truckers had long been the enemy of both treents and cyclists. While treents are not quick to judgment or action, I had tried to reason with a trucker once. The trucker insisted that treents had been demanding to take away their jobs. I explained that the treent moral code was to stay out of the human world unless we had no choice. The trucker insisted that the woods were intent on destroying the lives of truckers, so they had no choice but to destroy the woods. I asked "How do you know this is true?" And the trucker spat on me and shouted, "Another one playing dumb!"

However unconsidered, I understood why this individual would treat me this way if he believed this was true. In all of my decades, I have seen that well-intentioned misconceptions can lead a person into myriad ways of causing harm. But I felt that I knew the truth about the place I had lived all my life. After more misconceptions were dumped on me, I began to wonder aloud, "Who fed you so many lies?" I withdrew from interacting with humans for a time, wondering if they were all this way. I didn't think it concerned me anyway.

But now I knew what I had to do. With one eye on the misled foot soldiers of the petropatriarchy, I noticed a utility bicyclist with long, spiky pink hair over a fearless facial expression and decked out with a milk crate, rusty fenders, "car slayer" back patch, and a flatbed cargo trailer. They were moving at an inspired pace and slowed only due to the cracks in the pavement.

"There is trouble brewing on the horizon," I boomed.

"Huh?" the bicyclist responded, not realizing that a tree was talking to them from 50 feet up.

"I can see far into the distance. A renegade brigade of truckers is amassing. It is clear that they are up to something foul. And worse, headed this way. I see that you are a slayer. Is it so?"

The cyclist wordlessly nodded, dismounted, and entered a meditative stance after producing a comm from their back pocket.

I began calling out to each passing bicyclist, warning them of the dangers ahead. Some ignored me, but many were moving slowly enough to be curious and speak with the "talking tree," as one called me.

As a number of bicyclists remained nearby, it helped others to stop and see that there was a commotion. Before long, one had the idea to begin collecting the shattered pieces of my gigantic bicycle frame, sharpening the steel into tacking strips.

"Clever," I said. "Cars appear so indestructible, yet they are so feeble. So easily turned into immovable scrap metal. They act like they live forever, but try to find one as old as a treent."

The first bicyclist reported that they had heard news reports where the truckers had said that they were going to drive around pointlessly, protesting something or nothing—it was unclear. They had amassed fuel and were planning for the long haul of who knows what type of nonsense.

I recalled more about previous encounters with these types. The thing that upset me most is that they didn't have clear messaging or demands. It seemed like they had been hoodwinked by the powerful to do their bidding. They were victims too, but in every moment, any bad situation needs to be contained.

I remembered a time that a thorn growing on one of my vines had accidentally dangled into my tire, puncturing it. I had been briefly disheartened, but with the help of my trusty patch kit, I was back on the road in ten minutes. I hadn't even been late to my destination. I marveled at how reliable my steel horse had been for so many years. I felt a kinship with these human bicyclists. I had never paid them much mind before, to be honest. When our planet was more populated with them, it had seemed like they had such a short life cycle. Now, there are fewer of them and they have fewer annoying habits.

One of the bicyclists had the idea to obtain the element of surprise on the truckers before they had sight lines on us.

Everyone hid themselves and their bicycles behind various trees while I surveyed the situation.

The trucks drew nearer. There were about 60 of them, just pointlessly burning fuel. I felt a righteous anger well up inside of me as they closed in on our location.

"*Now!*" I bellowed, and the bicyclists emerged from behind dozens of trees and under the foliage to flip over fourteen rows of tacking strips made of found materials, revealing nature's spikes—sharpened to perfection. The tips gleamed, even through the smoggy atmosphere. Yet, from their distorted view, the truckers didn't see it coming. The first one drove across at full speed, puncturing four tires. The next tried to change lanes and soon suffered a similar fate. The third attempted to head into the lane intended for oncoming traffic and lost control, flipping the truck's trailer and skidding to a halt on its side. Now, all six lanes in both directions were completely blocked.

As the confused truck drivers angrily got out of their cabs and attempted to figure out what had happened, I instructed all of the bicyclists to climb to the tops of my branches and wiggled my roots, causing a series of tremors a mile deep into the ground.

Remembering a trick that my grandmother had taught me, I made my eyes a glowing red and bellowed "*Go back to where you came and take your garbage with you!*"

Bewildered and terrified, the truckers scrambled back into the remaining trucks and made a hasty departure. We rejoiced, knowing that they'd return but thinking that we could create new, superior engineering and hone our critical thinking skills to have the most fun every day.

I was not, however, prepared for my next surprise. The concrete had cracked, and my roots were free. My bonds were broken. Disrupting so much concrete so deep into the earth had released the surface's grip upon me. Even with my newly enlarged body, I could move freely again and slowly walked back to my orchard to plant the next wave of saplings.

SELF-PORTRAIT WITH A BICYCLE
⌁KATHRYN REESE⌁

The thing about bicycles is the limited amount of space for luggage. Unwieldy parcels dangle from handlebars, unbalanced loads in your backpack destabilize, dig into your spine. You need to slow down, find the curb cut, and use the footpath to stop, rearrange your load, and take a swig of isotonic orange rehydration solution.

Instead of a solid metal frame, dream up a bike that is poly pipes filled with water circulated by the turning of pedals. There could be growth, biofilms adhering to those poly pipes: green algae, cyanobacteria, and tiny soft-shelled nymphs—organic filtration to keep the water clean. Consider an interface at the handlebars: invisible hyphae extending through pores, onto the cyclist's bare skin, penetrating the space between epithelial layers. Hyphae soaking up mineral salt and sweat before it beads on her forehead.

This cyclist has no need to carry water in sterile plastic bottles. The water circulating through the machine flows into her hands. She has no thirst and no need for thirst. Those rigid boxes containing squares of soft bread and cheese that rub your back? She has a whole phylogenetic tree beneath her, devoted to her! Her diet is the organic decay at her fingertips, nymphs gather offerings of expired algae and castaway shells for her sustenance. Nitrogen, calcium, iron: all exchanged for her sweet salt.

The delicate architecture of her bloodstream molds to a new shape. The unwalled nest of her tangled DNA integrates the ancient code of the algae—she learns to photosynthesize. The tips of her wild hair, the nape of her neck, the line of her back where her T-shirt rises, these places glow, grow soft and green. Her need for air expands her lungs, pressing them into the tissue of her now disused liver. Like a fish, she moves also as she sleeps, this perpetual pedaling growing her hips wide, her thighs mighty, her buttocks deep, muscular, strong.

She had a destination, once, but it has been forgotten. She only rides, rides for the joy of the open bitumen, the corrugated dirt, the narrow forest path. All she desires is more, more and faster, as the nymphs feel the rush of current, shed their shells, and swim through hyphae-capillary tunnels and chasms of great veins, seeking the cave of her pelvis, to nest, awaiting metamorphosis at the right phase of the moon.

Faster, more and faster. Exquisite balance, divine speed. She pedals, taking no heed of mountain slopes or rain, the entire cycle sustained by pelvic ligaments that stretch to allow the oscillation of weight in response to the curve of the path. Exquisite balance, divine speed, the slip of tire through a slick of damp leaves, the leap over root, the skid around a fallen branch, the impact: tire, rock, knee, dirt, shoulder, head, dust, loam.

Silence.

On her knees, she spits into the dirt. With a torn hand she stirs a paste of mud, applies it to the cracks in the frame where green water beads and drips. A temporary seal.

It has been so long since she's been grounded. She shakes, sways as she rises to upright, and when she mounts she wobbles as a child on her first ride. She has not noticed her own skin, torn open and the smudge of dirt caught in the congealing blood.

You screw the plastic cap back on your rehydration drink, adjust your load, and pedal off the sidewalk, onto the asphalt, towards home.

CONTRIBUTORS

Amanda McNeil (she/her) is a queer woman who writes sci-fi and fantasy. Her work has been featured in *Decoded Pride*, *Solarpunk Magazine*, and the *Last Girls Club*. She has also published three novellas—*Waiting for Daybreak* (a woman finding sobriety while surviving the zombie apocalypse), *Bloemetje* (a space fantasy, queer-inclusive retelling of *Thumbelina*), and *Ecstatic Evil* (grumpy/sunshine paranormal romance). She currently lives in New England in the United States with her husband and their talkative tortie. You may find her online at OpinionsOfAWolf.com/publications.

Beatrice Toothman lives in the Central Valley with her fabulous spouse, Nick, and their cadre of rescue critters. She loves plants so much she tattooed an entire garden on her arm so she'd never go a day without flowers. When she's not pedaling around the neighborhood with her trusty bird-watching BFF, a senior chiweenie named Daisy, you can find her teaching reading and early literacy skills to kids and writing reviews for *City Book Review*.

Cass Wilkinson Saldaña is a writer, game designer, and librarian living on Narragansett land in Providence, Rhode Island. Their work follows themes of trans and queer embodiment, nonhuman subjectivity, and defiant play. You can follow their work at cass-ws.com.

Ella P. Francis is a writer of speculative and historical fiction residing in southern Pennsylvania. She is particularly fond of resurrecting the stories of strong women from history, folklore, and myth. Follow her on TikTok @ella_p_francis and Twitter @EllaPFrancis.

J.D. Harlock is an Eisner-nominated American academic pursuing a doctoral degree at the University of St. Andrews, whose writing has been featured in the *Cincinnati Review*, *Strange Horizons*, *Nightmare Magazine*, the *Griffith Review*, *Queen's Quarterly*, and New York University's Library of Arabic Literature.

Jennifer Lee Rossman (they/them) is a queer, disabled, and autistic author and editor from the land of carousels and Rod Serling. Their work has been featured in dozens of anthologies, and they are one of the editors of *Mighty: An Anthology of Disabled Superheroes*. Find more of their work on their website http://JenniferLeeRossman.blogspot.com and follow them on Twitter @JenLRossman.

After only 28 years as a trade book publisher, **Joe Biel** recently learned that fiction isn't factually inaccurate, it's emotionally true. Joe is the author of dozens of books, including *A People's Guide to Publishing* and the *Autism Relationships Handbook*, but has never written about talking trees before.

Kathryn Reese lives in South Australia. She works in medical science and enjoys road trips, long walks, and collaborative art experiments. Her poetry can be found in *JAKE*, *miniskirt mag*, and ecopoetic destinations such as *Paperbark Journal* and *Kelp Journal*. Her flash fiction "The Principal and the Sea," published by *Glassworks*, received a Best of the Net nomination.

By day, **Kathryn Reilly** helps students investigate words' power; by night, she resurrects goddesses and ghosts, spinning new speculative tales. Sometimes she even tells the truth. Enjoy poetry in *Shadow Atlas*, *A Flight of Dragons*, and *Last Girls Club*, and fiction in *Seaside Gothic*, *Bikes, the Universe, and Everything*, *Beneath the Yellow Lights*, and *Fish Gather to Listen*. Her rescue mutts hear all the stories first. When she's not working or writing, you can find her rewilding suburban spaces. Follow @KateCanWrite or visit KateCanWrite.com.

Kelley Tai is a speculative fiction writer and poet based in New Jersey. Her poem, "As a, I want to, so I can," has been nominated for this year's Aurora Award. In her free time, she likes to cuddle with her two kitties and play around with mechanical keyboards. You can find her list of publications and social media accounts on KelleyTai.com.

Lisa Timpf is a retired HR and communications professional who lives in Simcoe, Ontario. Lisa's speculative fiction has appeared in *NewMyths*, *Tails From the Front Lines 2: The Thin Blue Line*, *Home for the Howlidays*, *Cosmic Crime*, and other venues. Lisa's collection of speculative haibun poetry, *In Days to Come*, is available from Hiraeth Publishing. You can find out more about Lisa's writing at LisaTimpf.blogspot.com.

Marta Pelrine-Bacon grew up on a Florida lake and wandered around reading until she landed in Texas. She writes stories, makes art, and does her best to handle life, the universe, and everything. Her work in its various forms can be found on Patreon, Instagram (@mapelba), Substack, and at MartaPelrineBacon.com.

CREATE THE WORLD YOU WANT TO SEE AT MICROCOSM.PUB

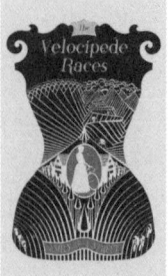

MORE FEMINIST BICYCLE SCIENCE FICTION: